HER HOPEFUL HEART
BOOK 40 THE AMISH BONNET SISTERS

SAMANTHA PRICE

Copyright © 2024 by Samantha Price

All rights reserved.

No part of this book may be reproduced in any form or by any electronic or mechanical means, including information storage and retrieval systems, without written permission from the author, except for the use of brief quotations in a book review.

CHAPTER 1

$\mathcal{D}$ebbie's eyes fluttered open to a dimly lit room, and before she could register where she was, her heart leaped into her throat. Cherish was hovering inches from her face, her eyes bright and concerned.

"Cherish!" Debbie gasped. "You nearly scared the living daylights out of me!"

"I'm sorry," Cherish replied, her lips quirking into a smile. "I didn't mean to startle you. I was seeing if you were awake."

"My eyes would've been open if I was awake."

Cherish laughed. "Sorry, Debbie. I just thought... we must do something to cheer you up today."

From the floor, a sleepy mumble interrupted their conversation. Favor sat up, rubbing her eyes. "I agree with Cherish. It will be too depressing if you stay home today. You've got to get out and do something."

Then, all the girls started waking up. Wilma's

daughters were in the room, including Krystal and Bliss. There was barely a square inch of floor where there wasn't someone sleeping.

Debbie pulled the quilt higher around her as the previous day's events replayed in her mind: the humiliation, the sorrow, and the abandonment by Fritz. "I don't feel like doing anything right now. If I go anywhere, people will talk about what happened."

Bliss put her arms over her head and stretched. "We understand. But you can't put your life on hold forever. You've gotta keep moving forward."

"I just... I never imagined waking up here, in Wilma's house, after... everything," Debbie said, her voice shaky. "I thought today I would've been in my new home with Fritz and starting a new life."

"Even the mention of his name makes me cross. I can't believe what he did to you," Mercy grumbled.

A moment of silence fell over the room. Then, Cherish's face lit up with an idea. "Why not move into the house that *Mamm* said was from Levi? It's just sitting there, waiting for a family to make it their home. Why not make it a home for you and Jared?"

Debbie bit her lip as she thought about it. She did need some kind of distraction.

Favor nodded eagerly, getting up from the mattress. "It's a great idea! It would help if you moved in there before we go home. We can help you get settled in and make it cozy for Jared. We can find a tree for that birdhouse he gave you."

Debbie hesitated, torn between the comfort of the familiar and the unknown. "I don't know..."

"It's a fresh start, Debbie. A place free of yesterday's memories. Somewhere you and Jared can create happier memories. If you stay here, it might be depressing," Bliss said.

Favor added, "You won't be alone. We'll be right by your side every step of the way. Cherish and I won't go home until you're all moved in. Right, Cherish?"

"Right." Cherish gave a nod. "We can stay for a few more days. Even if Ruth has to go home before us, we can hire a car to take us back."

Debbie blinked back tears. "I really need to talk with Fritz to find out…"

"There's no excuse," Mercy snapped.

"I still love him. I can't just switch my feelings off."

Honor's response was a little calmer. "He left you that note, and there's no doubt that the note was from him. So what more is there to be said?"

"Don't speak with him, Debbie. He'll only hurt you further," Bliss said.

"They're all right," Cherish announced. "Why he did what he did doesn't matter. It says everything!"

"I don't want to make any big decisions right now, but I was expecting a huge change in my life, and now… it's just the same as it always was."

Cherish started folding blankets. "That's right, so you can still have that huge change you were building up to. You must fly the nest, Debbie, just like I did when I left for the farm."

Debbie looked at the young woman she felt was the most sensible. "What do you think, Honor?"

"I agree that you might feel better if you do that," Honor said.

"Okay," Debbie whispered. "But I'll have to ask Wilma what she thinks. I don't even know if I should be making decisions like this right now."

"She'll miss you, but she'll understand," Cherish said.

Debbie's mind drifted back to the humiliation of Fritz leaving her at the altar. She didn't know if she would ever get over it. "Maybe I should move to another town where no one knows me."

Cherish moved closer, placing an arm around her. "It's not your fault. People will talk, yes, but in time, it will pass. No one will think badly of you. It's Fritz who'll be the one everyone is upset with."

Favor added, "And if anyone says anything unkind, they'll have to answer to me."

Debbie shook her head. "They won't say anything; they'll just pity me. If I stay here, everything will remind me of him. How do I move on from that?"

"One day at a time. Each step, each breath, will get a little easier. And remember, you have us. We'll be by your side through all of it. That is until we go home, but you'll feel much better by then," Bliss said.

Favor chimed in, "Think about Jared, too. He'll need a strong mother; you're the best mother he could ask for. Let's focus on the future and its joy for you both."

"Does it seem bad? Yes, and we all know how you must feel, but concentrate on other things. You'll find another man, a better man." Mercy shook her head. "I knew he wasn't right for you and saw something like this happening. I tried to say it to you, but there's only so much a person can warn another person."

Cherish glared at Mercy. "Oh, Mercy, you say that now, but you couldn't have seen it coming."

Mercy opened her mouth to argue back, but Honor got in first. "Let's not argue about who predicted it or not. We all have to support Debbie today, and this is not how to do it."

Debbie nodded slowly, taking in all the opinions. She knew she couldn't hide forever, and with the support of her dear friends, maybe she could find the strength to face the world again.

Favor stood up, stretching. "How about some breakfast? I'm starving."

Cherish chuckled. "Only you could think of food at a time like this."

Favor put a hand on her belly. "I can't help it. I'm eating for two now."

They all laughed, and even Debbie managed a smile.

Once they had changed into their day clothes, they went downstairs, the scent of fresh bread and brewing coffee filling the air.

Debbie found Jared quietly engrossed in his drawing, scribbling away at his little corner table. She kissed the top of his head, and he didn't even look up when she said good morning.

Wilma was over the stove, flipping pancakes. "Debbie, how are you feeling this morning?"

Debbie gave a weak smile, sitting at the table with the others. "I'm okay. As good as can be expected."

Wilma stared at Debbie a little harder. "Did you sleep well?"

"Yes, no. I don't know how. Sleep hasn't made me feel much better, but I suppose things will get easier with time… once people forget what happened. Once it's just a dim memory for all of us."

Wilma turned back to the pancakes. "Most people would've forgotten already. People are interested in their own lives mostly."

Favor and Cherish agreed, but Debbie knew it wasn't so. There would be letters being written and phone calls made. People would be talking about this for years to come, not only in their community but in Fritz's as well.

"Debbie has an idea she wants to discuss with you, *Mamm*," Cherish said.

"Yes?"

Debbie wasn't sure where to start. "First, I need some of those delicious-looking pancakes."

"Me too." Favor looked over at Jared. "You're quiet this morning. Got no 'good mornings' for anyone?"

Jared looked up as though he had only just noticed they were there. "Good morning, people."

They heard the front door open and close at that moment, and then there were footsteps.

Ada burst into the kitchen. "Debbie!" she exclaimed,

rushing over to embrace her. "How are you holding up?"

"Ada, slow down." Cherish jumped up and pulled out a chair for Ada.

"Oh, hush, Cherish." Ada shook her head and continued hugging Debbie.

"I'm fine, Ada, thanks for asking," Debbie eventually responded as she patted Ada's arm.

Ada then sat down in the seat Cherish had offered.

"Where is Harriet?" Favor asked, looking around.

"She's still sleeping. She'll be over later," Ada announced.

"What? She never sleeps this late," Favor squawked.

Ada grinned. "Maybe she's enjoying the break from doing all your housework and cooking."

"Possibly, but I hope she doesn't get into a lazy pattern. We'll have a baby to raise soon. There'll be no time for sleeping in." Favor's lips turned down at the corners.

"You and Simon will have a baby to raise," Ada pointed out. "Harriet will not—"

"Harriet wants to play a part. She said so," Favor blurted out.

Ada gave Favor a disapproving look and then stared at Debbie. "I got the number of where Fritz's mother is staying, and I spoke with her."

Debbie's eyes opened wide. "Is he coming back?"

Everyone looked over at Ada waiting to hear the news.

CHAPTER 2

*A*da shrugged her shoulders. "I hope it will make you feel better to know that Fritz's mother is as shocked and humiliated as we are. She had no idea he'd pull something like this."

Debbie sighed. "It doesn't make it easier if people are shocked or whatever. So, she has heard from him?"

"At least know you're not the only one he deceived," Bliss said.

"I don't know why you'd ask or even care if he's coming back, Debbie." Cherish shook her head.

Debbie bit her lip. She was cross, but at the same time, she needed answers.

"It sounds like you'd take him back, Debbie, would you?" Wilma stared at Debbie.

After a moment, Debbie cleared her throat to speak, but before she could, Wilma set down the pancakes in the middle of the table and then gave Jared his own serving.

Debbie eventually gave her answer. "I would like to talk with him to find out why he did what he did."

Favor grunted. "You're so nice, Debbie. Way too nice. I would be telling him a few things. I wouldn't be askin' anything."

"She loves him, that's why," Bliss said.

"Yeah, well, she'll get over it," Mercy commented.

"This looks delicious, Wilma. I've eaten, but I'll watch you all eat," Ada remarked.

After they'd said their silent prayers of thanks for the food, Wilma looked up at Debbie. "You know his number. You could call and speak with him directly if you have questions."

Debbie shook her head. "I don't know if that's a good idea. Instead of leaving that note, he would've talked if he wanted to."

"So would you take him back if he apologized?" Ada asked.

Cherish nearly choked on her pancake, and Favor had to pat her on the back. Everyone looked over, concerned, and Cherish quickly took a mouthful of water. "Are you serious, Ada? Apologize? Take him back?"

"It's Debbie's choice, Cherish." Bliss looked over at Debbie. "I'd be interested to hear your answer. Debbie, would you take him back if he realized he made a dreadful mistake and was sorry?"

"I don't know. It depends. It's just so sad. It'll take me a while to realize it's just me and Jared again."

"We're still here for you, all of us," Ada said.

"Thanks. I know that."

Cherish nudged Debbie. "You were going to talk with *Mamm* about something?"

"What is it?" Wilma asked, staring at Debbie.

"Well, there's something I've been thinking about. Well, I haven't been thinking about it for long. Cherish suggested it."

"Go on," Wilma said.

"The house from *Onkel* Levi, I'm considering moving in there. I'd like to hear what you think about the idea."

Wilma froze, and then, with her fork, she lifted a pancake onto her plate. "Move there now, you mean?"

"Yes. I thought... It's just a thought," Debbie hastened to add.

Wilma took a deep breath. "I'll miss you terribly, Debbie and Jared. But perhaps it's time you made your own way, build your own life."

"And now might be just the time to do it." Ada nodded.

Krystal's eyebrows shot up. "Are you sure about this, Debbie? I'll miss you. It won't be the same here."

Debbie knew that Krystal and Jed would probably soon marry, and then she'd be there in the house with just Wilma. "I do feel I need a fresh start. I had my mind set on a different beginning, but this could be good, too."

Ada placed a comforting hand on Debbie's. "It'll give you something else to turn your attention to. It's a brave step and, perhaps, the right one."

"Let's go check it out and see what needs to be done over there," Favor blurted out. "We could all go over and give it a good clean. Except not me because I shouldn't be exposed to dust in my condition, but I can see what needs doing."

Ada shook her head at Favor. "I'm not going to even comment on that. *Jah,* I will. You're pregnant, Favor, not ill."

"There's where you're wrong. I have been ill. I've had morning sickness. Just ask Harriet, and she'll tell you."

Then Debbie hesitated momentarily, the voices of doubt whispering in her ear. But looking around at the faces of her loved ones, she felt a glimmer of hope spark within her. "I think I'm going to do it. I need to take this step for myself and Jared."

"Great!" Favor clapped her hands together.

Jared looked up from his drawing. "Are we moving, *Mamm?*"

Debbie walked over and bent down. "Yes. We will start fresh in a new home, just the two of us."

Jared's eyes shone with excitement. "Will I have a new room?"

"Yes, you will."

"Can I paint it blue?"

Debbie chuckled. "Yes, you can have a blue room. I don't know if I'll let you paint, but someone will paint it for you."

The mood in the room lightened considerably, and the group began to discuss the logistics of the move.

Ada promised to rope in some of the community's young men to help with heavy lifting. Wilma grinned, knowing Ada was thinking about Gabe. The problem was there would be very little heavy lifting.

Cherish began listing the things that would need to be packed and moved while Favor eagerly offered to make curtains for the new house.

"Wait. Does it need curtains?" Mercy asked. "I can make them too. They need straight sewing, and I can sew straight."

"I never took too much notice of the curtains," Debbie confessed.

"We must wait until Harriet gets here. I'm sure she'd like to come too," Ada said.

"I'm sorry I can't come, Debbie, but I have to go to work," Krystal said.

Jared grinned. "And I have to go to school unless…"

Debbie shook her head at Jared. "Yes, you have to go to school."

"That's not fair. I want to help."

"There will be plenty for you to do later when it's not a school day."

"Are we moving into the house Fritz showed us?" Jared asked.

The room fell silent as Debbie shook her head. "No. We're moving into a smaller one, and the size is just right for us."

Once breakfast was over, Ada and Wilma were alone in the kitchen while the young women were upstairs getting ready for the day ahead.

"It's so sad what happened," Wilma murmured, her fingers idly tracing patterns on the wooden table. "How is Debbie not staying in bed for a week? I would have locked myself away and cried."

Ada sighed. "It's Jared that keeps her going, I'm sure. But every time I look into her eyes, I see that shadow of pain. We need to do something, Wilma."

Wilma looked at her old friend, noting the determined glint in her eyes. "What do you have in mind?"

Ada pondered, then said, "She needs another man. Someone kind, strong, and understanding. Someone who'll treat her right and be a father to Jared."

Wilma raised her eyebrows. "I agree, but I think it's too soon for that. A broken heart needs time to mend."

Ada huffed, rolling up her sleeves and stepping over to the sink. "I'm just saying love is a great healer as well. And with the right person, she can find happiness again. The sooner, the better."

"Rushing into another relationship isn't the answer." Wilma shook her head.

Ada glanced over at Wilma. "You're wrong."

"We'll have to agree to disagree then," Wilma said.

"I think we will." Ada started the water for the washing up while Wilma brought over the dirty plates.

"I have to stop myself from feeling angry toward Fritz," Wilma commented.

"As so we all." Ada immersed her hands in the sudsy water, and then her gaze was drawn to what was happening on the other side of the window. Gabe was by the apple trees, carefully examining something in his hands. "Gabe..." Ada breathed, her face brightening with an idea. "Look at him, Wilma. He might not be single for long. Debbie should waste no time."

Wilma stood beside her. Gabe was a handsome figure; his shirt sleeves rolled up, revealing solid forearms. "I agree, he'll be a good catch for someone. He's hardworking and polite. He seems to be diligent, too. He hasn't missed a meeting since he's been here."

Ada continued washing dishes without taking her eyes off Gabe. "I think he's kind-hearted, and we know two of his brothers quite well."

Wilma nodded. "Yes. Jed and Malachi are good young men."

"I've seen how Gabe and Debbie get along. If she had met Gabe first, she wouldn't have given Fritz a second thought."

"Oh, Ada, you can't say that because you don't know. Gott has His own plans, and we can't predict them."

Ada sighed, wringing out a cloth. "I know, I know. But it wouldn't hurt to nudge things along, right?"

Wilma chuckled. "You and your match-making ideas. Just promise me you won't rush things, jah?"

Ada smirked. "That's a promise I might not be able to keep, so I won't make it. But one thing's for sure. With Gabe around, Debbie's future looks a lot brighter. I can feel it."

Wilma smiled, glancing back out the window at Gabe, who was walking toward the house with a basket of apples. "Maybe you're right. Only time will tell."

CHAPTER 3

There was too much talking and too many opinions flying around in Debbie's room. Everyone had their own ideas on how Debbie should move forward. Some said she should contact Fritz to tell him how she felt, and others said he didn't even deserve her to speak with him.

She had to get away by herself so she could think about her next move without feeling pressured this way or that. She slipped outside without anyone noticing.

Debbie had been meticulously working on hitching the buggy, trying to think when Gabe approached. His footsteps drew her attention, and she turned to find him watching her, an expression of sympathy in his eyes. The soft clinking of the harness was the only sound between them before he finally spoke.

"I'm truly sorry about what happened, Deb," he said as he placed a bucket of apples on the ground.

"Thank you, Gabe," she replied softly.

He hesitated momentarily, then asked, "Did you have any inkling he was going to... do that?"

Debbie shook her head, her lips pressed into a thin line. "No idea at all. He told me the night before that his mother wasn't coming. He said that made him sad. Maybe our conversation didn't go as he had hoped, or perhaps it reminded him of how his mother and I never got along that well. I'm not certain." She sighed, her fingers tightening around a brass harness buckle. "Anyway, it's over now."

Gabe shifted uncomfortably. "Have you heard from him?"

The question brought a bitter smile to her face, though she kept her voice steady. "No, I haven't."

Gabe stepped closer, relieving her of the task of hitching the buggy. "You know, it's Fritz's loss. Truly."

Debbie looked up at him, taken aback by the intensity of his words. "I appreciate you saying that."

Gabe finished with the harness and turned fully to face her. "Whatever reasons Fritz had, he made a grave mistake. One he'll likely regret."

Debbie took a deep breath, steadying herself. "I hope I'll come to see it that way. Right now, it's just... raw."

Gabe nodded, his eyes searching hers. "How is Jared taking it?"

"He's fine. If he's upset, he's doing a good job covering it up. He was looking forward to having a father, though. I know that much for certain."

"Well, you don't miss what you never had."

She was surprised to hear him say that since he had a father. Then, she recalled hearing that his father might not have been the father he had hoped for. "Only time will tell if it's affected Jared beyond what he shows. Most of the time, whatever is in his head comes right out of his mouth."

"I'm sure he'll be fine. He's got you, and the whole thing hasn't taken him out of his routine."

Debbie nodded, but now had a new worry. How would Jared cope with the change of living in a new place? "You're right there. He does like his routine."

"If you or Jared need anything, anything at all, just ask."

"Thank you, Gabe," she whispered.

"There," he said, ensuring everything was secure. "All set for you."

Debbie offered a grateful smile. "Thank you, Gabe."

"Just doing my part," he replied with a modest shrug. Their eyes met for a moment, a silent acknowledgment passing between them.

"Where are you heading today?" he asked.

"We're all going to look at a house that Wilma gave me. Wilma's late husband, Levi, was my uncle. He owned a few houses that he rented out. Wilma inherited them, and she's given one to me. So, I've decided to move into it."

He rubbed his jaw. "You're moving?"

"I am."

"It's not too far away, I hope."

She smiled and was flattered that he seemed to care. "It's only a few minutes away."

"Let me know if you need help moving."

Debbie blinked in surprise. "That's very kind of you, Gabe. I might take you up on that."

"You shouldn't be doing anything alone, especially not now."

She hesitated, touched by Gabe's offer. "I have my friends helping. But thank you. I'll let you know if we need an extra pair of hands."

Gabe looked down, a hint of color flushing his cheeks. "I just... well, I want you to think of me as a friend."

There was a beat of silence. Debbie studied him, taking in his sincere expression, the depth of emotion in his eyes. It wasn't pity; it was genuine care. "You're a very kind man, Gabe."

Gabe cleared his throat, clearly a bit taken aback by her acknowledgment. "I'm glad to hear you think so."

Debbie took a deep breath, feeling the weight of the moment. "I need all the friends I can get."

He nodded. "Fritz's choices don't reflect on you. And if you ever need someone to remind you of that, I'm here."

She smiled faintly, unsure of what he meant. It could be taken a few ways, but now wasn't the time to analyze anything. "I'll keep that in mind."

They stood there for a moment longer. A gentle wind rustled the leaves of the nearby trees, breaking the silence.

"Sounds like the wind's picking up. It would be best to get going before it gets too strong," Gabe advised.

"Yes," Debbie replied, glancing toward the open road. "We're just waiting for Harriet to show up, and then we'll all go together."

Gabe stepped away from the buggy. "Remember, just give me a shout if you need help. My hours here at the orchard are flexible."

Debbie nodded. "I will."

With a final nod, Gabe picked up his bucket and walked back into the orchard.

CHAPTER 4

*D*ebbie took a moment to steady herself. Gabe had made her feel wanted, whereas, with Fritz, she had always felt pushed aside.

She had hardly taken a few steps to the house when she heard the rapid patter of footsteps. Looking up, she saw Cherish and Favor's faces flushed with excitement as they rushed to her.

"What was that all about?" Favor asked, her eyes gleaming with curiosity.

"What?" Debbie knew what she meant but didn't want to be the subject of speculation or gossip more than she was already.

"Gabe!" Cherish blurted out. "Something's going on there, I can tell."

"Oh, is that why Fritz left? He knew you liked Gabe? He was stepping back. How romantic. Now you're torn between two men. Oh, Debbie, why didn't you tell us."

Cherish elbowed her sister. "That's not what happened." Then Cherish looked at Debbie. "Wait. Is that what happened, Debbie?"

Debbie let out a small sigh. "Nothing is going on. Gabe just offered to help me move. I hardly know him. I just met him a few weeks ago."

Favor's eyebrows rose. "Looked like you'd known him longer. Besides, you know when you meet the man you're meant to marry."

Cherish eagerly added, "I didn't even like Malachi when I first met him."

Favor put her hands on her hips and stared at Cherish. "I'm talking about most people. That's the way most people fall in love."

Debbie took a deep breath. "Please don't argue. I can't deal with that today. Gabe's just being a good neighbor and a friend."

Cherish wrapped an arm around Debbie's shoulders, pulling her into a side hug. "A pretty nice-looking friend if you ask me."

Debbie let out a small chuckle, cheeks turning a shade pinker. "Oh, stop it."

Favor giggled, joining the group huddle. "You have to admit, Debbie. Gabe has eyes for you."

Debbie playfully swatted at her. "Alright, alright, enough teasing. Besides, I've got a lot on my plate, and dating isn't one of them. I want to focus on having a normal life again."

Cherish tilted her head, giving Debbie a scrutinizing look. "Who said anything about dating? We're just pointing out the obvious. There's chemistry."

Favor nodded, a mischievous glint in her eyes. "The way he looked at you is not just any look. That's *the* look."

Debbie exhaled dramatically, feigning exasperation. "Okay, detectives. Can we please move on from my non-existent love life?"

Cherish released her. "We'll move on for now. But only because we have that house to look at. But trust me, this isn't over."

Favor winked. "Not over at all."

Together, the trio headed inside, their laughter echoing around them. But behind her playful protestations, Debbie couldn't help but wonder if there might be a hint of truth to their teasing.

She had felt something just now. And if she felt something, had Gabe felt it too?

EVERYONE GOT busy packing the buggy with cleaning equipment. The plan was that once they assessed Debbie's new place, they'd give it a good clean.

Harriet arrived expecting a scene of devastation, but when she stepped into the living room, she was met with an entirely different scenario. All the girls were there, surrounded by a bustle of activity.

"What's going on?" Harriet asked.

Cherish grinned. "Debbie is moving house, probably."

Debbie nodded. "Good morning, Harriet. I think I will do it. It's time for a fresh start."

As they discussed the move, the gentle hum of a car's engine broke their conversation. Cherish rushed to the window to see a flash of red pulling up in the driveway. "It's Ruth!"

Cherish stepped out on the porch and waved to her. "Ruth, we're heading to Debbie's new place. Want to come?"

Ruth smiled as she glanced over at the buggies full of cleaning equipment. "Of course! I'd love to."

Cherish opened Ruth's passenger side car door. "Room for one more?"

Ruth laughed. "Sure. Hop in!"

When everyone got to Debbie's cottage, they noticed that some paint was peeling here and there, and the garden was full of weeds. But the house itself was solid. It could become a comfortable and cozy haven with some work and care.

"Wilma, look at the weeds. Isn't Carter looking after it?" Ada asked.

"He is, but we've had so much rain. I'll let him know to get the gardeners in."

"No need. We'll do it all," Ada assured her.

"It has potential," Mercy remarked, taking in the sight.

"I agree," Debbie whispered. "It can be a place of healing."

Honor put an arm around Debbie. "Let's go and check it out."

Together, the group entered the house.

The house's wooden floors creaked underfoot as the group dispersed into various rooms. Echoes of laughter and chatter filled the air as they explored the nooks and crannies of Debbie's soon-to-be sanctuary.

"Look at this!" Cherish called from one of the rooms. There was an old fireplace, its mantel decorated with intricate carvings of birds and flowers.

Favor, who had always had an eye for obscure design, clapped her hands with glee. "This could be the focal point of the room. Some cleaning, maybe a fresh coat of paint on the walls, and it'll be gorgeous."

Harriet had found the attic, gone up the stairs, and crawled into the small space. She called down, "There is some furniture up here. Some might be salvageable!"

"We'll look at that later," Ada called back.

Debbie, examining the kitchen, was already envisioning its transformation. "All that's needed is a fresh coat of paint on these cabinets."

Wilma pursed her lips in disapproval. "They look fine to me, but if you want a different color, we can paint it."

"Aw, *Mamm*, she just wants to make it her own," Cherish said.

"Then we should go to the store to choose some colors once you know what needs painting," Honor suggested.

As they explored and planned, Mercy pulled Debbie

aside. "Are you sure about this?" she whispered, eyes searching Debbie's. "You've never been in a house with just you and Jared. You might get lonely. Think of the night-time when Jared has gone to bed, and you're sitting alone in the darkness."

Debbie nodded, her determination firm. "I've made up my mind now that I've seen this house again. I can make a new life here. I'll get used to the solitude."

Overhearing their conversation, Ruth added, "And you won't be doing it alone. You have so many people around you."

Debbie smiled at Ruth and thanked her.

CHAPTER 5

An hour later, Ada, Wilma, and Harriet accompanied Debbie to the local hardware store. The store had that familiar smell of wood and paint that immediately filled one's senses upon entry. Ada led the way, eyes scanning the rows of paint cans and color samples.

"Something light and airy for the living room, perhaps?" Ada mused, picking up a color sample of pale blue. "But we want it to feel like home, too. Hmm. There's green with envy. Out of the blue."

Debbie looked over at Ada. "Are they the names of the colors?"

"No. I'm just thinking of sayings that have colors in them. I do love sayings."

"That's right she does," Wilma agreed with a laugh.

"White as a sheet. Once in a blue moon. Oh my, someone should employ me to come up with names for the paint." Ada chuckled at her own comment.

Debbie's eyes hovered over the samples, her heart swaying between shades of white and cream. "I want the place to be cozy, but not dark," she whispered, almost to herself, but the women around her nodded in understanding.

Meanwhile, back at Debbie's new place, the younger women had taken charge of the clean-up. Cherish directed the operations with a flourish as she marched from room to room.

"Measure twice, cut once," Cherish called out to the girls, who measured the windows for curtains.

"We're only measuring, not cutting," Favor called back.

"You say making curtains is just sewing a straight line," Cherish said to Favor after a mischievous glance, "but I've seen your 'straight' lines before. They could rival the winding roads of our town."

"I think Mercy said that, not me. Besides, we won't be making dresses, so you won't notice if it's a bit wavy in one or two places."

Mercy scowled at Cherish. "You're so mean."

"I'm just joking," Cherish said.

Ruth blinked rapidly. "Do we have time to make curtains? We do have to get home. I'm sure you're all missing your husbands."

Mercy grimaced. "Honor and I couldn't get away without our whole family coming with us. I didn't even think of just her and me coming alone."

"Next time, maybe," Honor said. "When we come for Debbie's next wedding."

"Or for Krystal's wedding," Mercy suggested. "That'll most likely come next, so everyone tells me."

The house was alive with activity, the sounds of cleaning and the occasional light banter echoing through the bare rooms. It was amid this bustling scene that Eli arrived, his presence marked by the soft clop of horse hooves on the gravel path.

The girls, seeing him from the window, waved him in. "Ada and Wilma are out with Debbie, picking paints and dreaming up new colors for the house," Mercy informed him.

Eli's face broke into a wide grin. "Moving in, is she?" he said with a chuckle. "Well, I think it's a great idea."

"Come in and take a look around," Cherish said.

Eli moved around the house energetically, his eyes keen for the little imperfections he could fix.

His gaze then fell upon the large birdhouse, a labor of love crafted by his hands and Jared's. He stepped outside, scanning the expanse of the yard for the perfect tree. "Needs to be sturdy," he murmured to himself. "Somewhere high enough for the birds to feel safe and where Debbie and Jared can see them from the window."

After a moment, he found a grand old oak with branches that spoke of strength and resilience. With a satisfied nod, he marked the spot in his mind.

By the time Ada, Wilma, and Harriet returned with Debbie, the windows had been measured, and the old curtains had been taken down, letting in more light and giving the rooms a different feel.

Debbie had made a purchase besides paint. It was a clock which she placed in the kitchen.

Wilma and Ada told everyone about Debbie's paint choices. She'd settled on a warm cream for the living room, a soft green for her bedroom, blue for Jared's, and yellow for the kitchen.

"Yellow for the kitchen?" Cherish exclaimed. "That'll be bright and cheerful, just like our Debbie."

Debbie smiled. "Thank you for being here, everyone. Even though I didn't get married, I'm so pleased to see everyone back here."

"We're glad to be back and to see you get settled in," Honor said and the others agreed.

They all kept working for a few more hours.

Ever mindful of the responsibilities that tethered her heart, Debbie glanced at a clock on the living room wall. "Someone needs to be home for Jared," she said, a twinge of concern threading her words. "He'll be wondering where we all are."

Ruth, who had been methodically cleaning the windows, laid down her cloth. "I'll go fetch him," she offered. "It'd be nice for him to see the house come to life."

"I'll come with you and show you where to go," Cherish said, wiping her hands on her apron. "A bit of a drive sounds wonderful after all this cleaning."

Ruth nodded, and together, they headed to the door, stepping out into the embrace of the afternoon sun.

CHAPTER 6

Jared had started walking home to Wilma's house when Ruth's car pulled up beside him. Cherish waved enthusiastically from the passenger seat. His face brightened when he realized he was going for a ride in a car. He ran to the car and got into the backseat.

"Your new house is getting all fixed up," Cherish announced as Jared buckled up. "It's going to be a special place; just wait and see."

Jared's eyes sparkled with excitement. "Can I see my room?"

"You'll see the whole house," Ruth assured him with a smile, catching his gaze in the rear-view mirror.

Back at the house, Eli was straightening up from inspecting the foundations when he heard the car return. He watched as Jared hopped out.

Eli knew that moment was right to fulfil a promise he and Jared had made together—the promise of

SAMANTHA PRICE

finding the perfect spot for the large birdhouse. Although they each thought it would be at a different house.

Eli waved Jared over and together they strolled around the yard, Jared's chatter filling the space between them. "I want to watch the birds from the kitchen window like we can with Aunt Wilma's birdhouse."

Eli nodded, his eyes sweeping over the trees until they landed on the tree he'd spotted earlier. "That one there." He pointed at it. "It's sturdy and tall; you can see it clear from the kitchen."

Jared's eyes followed Eli's gesture, and a wide grin spread across his face. "Yeah, that's perfect!"

"Next time, I'll bring a ladder to hang it high. The birds will have the best home in the whole yard."

Their moment of shared planning was gently interrupted by a more somber conversation. Eli looked down at Jared, his expression softening. "Do you understand what happened between your mom and Fritz?" he asked.

Jared's brow furrowed; the memory still sharp in his mind. "Fritz wrote a note, and everyone thought it was from me. I got the blame, but then they found out Fritz did it. Fritz didn't want to marry *Mamm,* so I must wait for a new father."

Eli's chuckle was a soft rumble. "You know, Jared," he began, "the best father isn't always the one you're born with. It's the one who steps up and loves you like his own. And you, young man, will have the best *Dat*. I'm sure of it."

Jared's eyes, so like Debbie's in their depth, looked up at Eli. "All the other boys in the class have a Dat. I'm the only one who has none."

Eli crouched down to meet Jared's gaze, his voice whispering of shared experience. "My father died when I was about your age. I grew up without one, and my *mamm* never married again. But let me tell you, Jared, that never stopped me from finding fathers in all the men who cared for me along the way."

Jared absorbed Eli's words, a thoughtful expression etching his features. "You got no *Dat* either?"

"No," Eli affirmed. "And I had a good life, filled with people who loved me. Just like you will."

Jared looked up at the tree with a faraway look in his eyes.

"Come on, young man, let's see how the house is shaping up."

As they stepped back into the house, the evidence of a day's hard work surrounded them. The walls were scrubbed and ready for painting, and the whole place smelled fresh and homely.

Jared ran to the kitchen window, pressing his face against the cool glass, looking at the big tree that would soon be home to his and Eli's birdhouse creation. Then, after he was satisfied he'd be able to watch the birds, he ran to find his room.

CHAPTER 7

They were all still busy at Debbie's new home when Ada had an important question. "What will we do for the evening meal, Wilma?"

Wilma wiped her hands on her apron. "Everyone will have to come back to my house for a meal. We've had no time to cook, but I'll find something."

"What shall we have?" Ada's question hung in the air, an invitation for suggestions.

A chorus of ideas bubbled forth as they discussed what food they could prepare quickly. Mercy suggested egg noodles; they were fast and always comforting. Honor's idea was a hearty vegetable soup, the kind that could be conjured from whatever was in the pantry. Harriet mentioned a tossed salad, crisp and fresh, the perfect counterpart to any leftovers.

The girls all offered to help, their voices overlapping in eager anticipation of the shared meal. Favor, whose culinary skills were often dubious, volunteered for salad duty, quipping that even she couldn't mess up washing lettuce.

"Many hands make light work," Ada said.

Wilma grinned at her. "Another saying?"

"Naturally."

"I'll buy us some desserts on the way back to your house, Wilma."

"Thank you, Ruth. Everyone loves desserts," Wilma said.

Eli, who had been quietly listening, leaned against the doorframe with a half-grin. "Am I invited even though I've done no work?"

Wilma laughed. "Eli, you know you're always welcome," she responded. "And if you're looking for odd jobs in the future, I'm sure Debbie will have many of them."

"I'll be glad to help in any way I can."

The group acknowledged the day's achievements with a final glance around Debbie's home.

They left the house in a convoy of buggies and Ruth's car and made their way to Wilma's house.

Arriving at Wilma's, the noodles were the first to be set on the stove. They decided on a little of everything. The soup came with a medley of vegetables—carrots, potatoes, onions, and celery—filling the pot with a rainbow of colors and flavors.

True to her word, Ruth returned with a selection of desserts from the local supermarket.

Samuel soon arrived with Mercy and Honor's families, and not long after that, Krystal came with Jed.

Someone had invited Gabe because he was there too.

When the meal was ready, the adults gathered around the large table, and all bowed their heads and said their silent prayers. The children did the same at their own table.

Once the prayers had been said, they passed dishes hand to hand, serving each other with the ease of family. The salad was a crisp contrast to the hot dishes, but only Samuel seemed interested in it.

The conversation got around to what Debbie would do about transportation.

"I noticed an outbuilding. I should've had a better look at it. Will it keep a horse?" Eli asked.

Debbie nodded. "I think it will. Does anyone know of a good horse for sale?"

"Take the one you've been using from here. And the buggy," Wilma insisted.

"No. I can't do that, Wilma. I'll get my own. I appreciate the thought, but I want to do that."

"Samuel, what about that one you bought from an auction last week?" Ada asked.

Samuel hung his head and mumbled, "I'm keeping that one."

Ada stared at him, blinking. "For what? We already have several."

Wilma chuckled. "Levi was like that. He loved his horses. They like collecting them."

Samuel picked up his glass and took a mouthful of soda. "I do have one I could spare."

"No, it's okay. I can buy one. I want to. Will someone come with me to the auction?" Debbie looked around at everyone.

"Why did the pony have trouble singing?" Stephen blurted out.

Mercy stiffened at hearing yet another joke.

"I don't know. Why?" Jonathon said.

"Because he was a little hoarse." Stephen laughed. "Get it? A little hoarse."

Jed chuckled, and so did a couple of other people.

"Stephen, Debbie asked a question, and you didn't allow anyone to answer," Ada said before she turned to Debbie. "I have a friend, and he would love to help you find a horse. I'll arrange it. Leave everything to me."

Debbie was relieved she wouldn't have to go alone. "Thank you, Ada, that would be lovely."

"Does this person know about horses?" Samuel asked. "Because I could take you, Debbie."

"Of course he does. The person I have in mind is very knowledgeable and he would love to go with you, Debbie," Ada said.

"Um, can I ask who it is?" Debbie said.

Samuel stared at his wife. "I'd like to know too."

"When's the next auction?" Ada asked.

"There's one on Friday," Eli said. "I'll go with you too, Debbie."

Ada frowned at Eli, but he didn't notice.

"Then I'll go too if you're going, Eli," Samuel stated. "Well, Ada, who is the person you've got in mind?"

"I'm not going to say who the person is just yet," Ada said.

"Just have this mystery person meet us here at nine on Friday, and then we'll all go together," Samuel said with a slight shake of his head.

"Thank you. I will feel better with lots of opinions." Debbie was a little disappointed that Gabe had just sat there in silence. Perhaps he didn't know much about horses.

"Anyone want to hear another joke?" Stephen asked.

"No!" Jonathon and Mercy said at the same time.

Stephen cleared his throat. "Okay. I'll save them for another time when I have an audience who appreciates them."

Wilma turned to Ada. "Stephen has jokes, and you have sayings, Ada. Do you have a saying about a horse?"

"I do. Let me think. You can lead a horse to water, but you can't make him drink."

Stephen quickly added, "Did you get that straight from the horse's mouth, Aunt Ada?"

"Please stop," Mercy whispered to him.

"Okay. I'll be quiet. It wasn't a joke though and I couldn't resist that one. Now, I have to tell you all something. I know we were going to stay longer, but we do have to leave tomorrow."

Mercy sighed. "And we're only finding out about this now?"

Jonathon nodded. "Sorry. You and Honor have been out all day, so it's been hard to talk. We've got cars coming at eight in the morning."

Honor shook her head. "We won't be able to help you with the house, Debbie. I'm so sorry."

"That's okay. I'm just glad you all saw it."

"I didn't see it," Stephen said.

"She meant Honor and me," Mercy told him.

"We have to go home?" Stephen's oldest asked from the children's table.

"Yes, we do. When you wake in the morning, it'll be time to go home."

"Aw, I wanted to stay longer."

The other boys agreed but didn't say anymore when they saw Ada glaring at them for speaking during the meal. Only the adults were permitted to do that.

"I hope you'll settle into the house, and you'll love it," Mercy said to Debbie.

"Thank you."

Stephen made another attempt at a joke about moving house, a pun about 'box-ing' the items that fell flat. Debbie saw the easy shrug off his shoulders as barely anyone laughed, a carefree gesture that somehow deepened the furrow in Mercy's brow.

When the meal was over, Debbie approached Mercy and took her aside.

CHAPTER 8

Debbie whispered to Mercy. "Don't be upset with Stephen. He's trying, Mercy. In his way, he's trying to lift everyone's mood. I'd do anything to have a husband who loved me. You have that. Please appreciate it."

Mercy managed a weak smile. "I know, Debbie. But sometimes, I need him to lift the load, not just the mood. You are on the outside looking in. It's not all that great."

"Talk to him about how you feel. Clear skies come after the hardest rains. Don't give up. You both love each other."

"I've tried talking, but he never listens. It's useless."

"Then try again. Sooner or later, he has to listen."

"Thanks, Debbie. With all you've got going on, I'm surprised you noticed what's happening between Stephen and me."

"You have confided in me about it, so that's probably why."

"Oh yeah. I forgot. Okay, I'll try again. Thanks." The two women exchanged a smile. Then Mercy breathed and motioned for Stephen to join her on the porch.

Outside, Stephen sat beside his wife, his smile fading as he took in her serious expression. "What's up?"

Mercy searched for the right words before she spoke. "Stephen, sometimes it feels like you don't see how much I struggle."

He blinked, the joy draining from his face, replaced with a dawning realization. "I thought I was helping in my own way. Making you laugh. Everyone feels better when they laugh and smile."

"It's not just about laughing with me, Stephen. It's about standing with me. Helping with the boys, and the house. There are so many odd jobs left undone. There are squeaky drawers and cupboard doors that don't shut. You don't ever listen to me. You keep telling me you'll do things tomorrow, but tomorrow never comes and those jobs aren't being done." The words once held back, now flowed like a river breaking through a dam.

Stephen took her hand, his laugh absent, his eyes earnest. "I didn't know. I thought I was doing enough. I'll do better, Mercy. I'll be better. But I work outside the home, and you work inside. Isn't that how it's meant to be?"

"Yes, but I work harder all day, and my day doesn't

stop until I fall asleep. I need a little help. Is that too much to ask?"

"I'll help more. You need to tell me what to do. I don't know what needs doing if you don't tell me."

"I'll tell you."

"Okay." He put his arm around Mercy. "Now, will you smile?"

"And less jokes. I'm not saying that you stop altogether. Just do it when it's the right time. Over dinner just now was not the right time."

"Okay. I can see that now. Not everyone has a sense of humor. What happened to Debbie has made me realize how blessed I am to have you."

Mercy was shocked to hear it. "Do you mean that?"

"Of course I do. It's not easy for people to find the right person to marry, but we found each other early on." He took her hand. "I want to be the best I can for you. What do I need to do?"

"Just be more aware of everything."

"That sounds wishy-washy, but I'll do my best."

"It's more important now than ever."

"Why's that?"

She put her hand over her belly and then looked up at him. "We're having another baby."

He gasped. "Are you serious, or are you joking now?"

"It's true, but don't tell anyone right now. There's too much going on. I haven't even told Honor. I told Favor, but she's so concerned about herself that she'll probably forget. I did tell her to keep it quiet for now and she agreed. Let's share the news later."

He drew her into a hug. "We're blessed, Mercy. Three boys. That's wonderful."

Mercy laughed. "Wait a minute. It might be a girl."

"Nope. Only boys in my family. I'm one of three boys, and it's more likely that it'll be another boy. I don't mind either way."

"I do. I want a girl."

"We'll have to wait and see." He let out a contented sigh.

There was a long road ahead, but Mercy felt like they were on the road together for the first time in a long time.

When Debbie saw Mercy and Stephen come back inside, she took the opportunity to be alone and slipped out onto the porch to breathe fresh air.

From the moment Debbie's world had fallen apart, she hadn't stopped. She appreciated everyone rallying around her, but it had given her little time to process the disaster.

As she settled into a porch chair, she couldn't help but feel a sense of relief amidst the turmoil. The opportunity to be alone, away from the sympathetic glances and well-meaning words, was calming.

It wasn't long before her thoughts turned to him—the man she had loved, trusted, and envisioned a future with. How could he have left her like that, without a word, without an explanation? Anger bubbled up inside her, mixed with a deep sense of betrayal. She had given him her heart; in return, he had left a gaping hole in her life.

Again, she replayed their last moments together, searching for any sign or hint of what was coming. But there was nothing - just the memory of his smile, his promises of forever, and his dreams of a life together. How could someone who professed to love her inflict such pain?

Debbie stood and moved closer to one of the poles that held the porch's roof. It was then that she noticed a figure leaning against the railing below. She let out a gasp.

CHAPTER 9

It was Gabe. He turned his head and looked up. "I'm sorry, I didn't mean to startle you," he apologized. "I just came out here for a moment."

"It's alright," she said. The sky overhead was a vast canvas of twinkling stars and velvety darkness, a reminder of the world's immense beauty and depth. She looked up, lost for a moment in God's celestial display. "The night sky makes you realize just how small you are."

Gabe stepped up beside her, following her gaze to the heavens. "Yes, it does." They stood side by side in comfortable silence, gazing upward.

After a moment, Gabe broke the quiet. "How was today at the new house?" His question was gentle, an invitation rather than an intrusion.

Debbie sighed, leaning back against the railing, gripping the weathered wood. "It's made me do a lot of thinking," she confessed. "I'm so blessed, Gabe. When I came here to Levi's house, I was lost and unwanted by my parents. I was pregnant with Jared, and my husband had died. He'd kept our marriage a secret, so no one even knew. Even at the funeral, I felt I couldn't admit we were married."

"Why was that?"

Even though it was so long ago, the disappointment that John had given her still gave her a knot in her stomach. "His parents would've been so upset, and I couldn't add the extra burden of them knowing their son was keeping such a secret."

"I understand. That sounds like a heavy burden."

"It was unbelievable." Now, another man had abandoned her. "If Levi hadn't taken me in, I don't know where I'd have ended up or where Jared would be."

"Levi sounds like a good man. I would've liked to have met him."

She smiled faintly, and the smile quickly faded. "Sometimes I feel like I'm just holding on, trying not to be swept away."

"That's what faith is, though, isn't it?" Gabe's voice was soft but sure. "It's holding on during the toughest times. And our part is getting up each morning, putting one foot in front of the other, even when the night has been too long."

Debbie nodded, her heart feeling the truth of his words. "I guess you're right. But it's not just me. It's all the people around me. Without them—without this community—I'd be lost."

"That's the beauty of this life we live," Gabe said, gesturing to Wilma's house, the sounds of the evening's celebration still audible through the walls.

Her eyes met his, and in them, she found an echo of her own determination. "I just worry about Jared. All of this has been hard on him, too."

"He's a brave boy," Gabe assured her. "And he has his mother's heart. He'll grow through this, just like you have. Kids are tougher than you think."

"I hope so." Debbie let out a long breath, feeling the tightness in her chest ease. "I just want to give him the world, you know? A place where he can feel safe, loved, and free to be himself. In many ways, he's not like other children."

"And you will," Gabe said with confidence. "You've started already with your new house. It's more than just walls and a roof. It's part of your future."

The future. The word resonated with her, a daunting and exhilarating promise. "I hope so," she said.

Gabe turned to face her fully, his hat now in his hands. "Hope is a powerful thing. It's the seed from which all good things grow. And from what I've seen tonight and how people react to you, you've planted plenty of good things."

Debbie's lips curved into a smile. "Thank you, Gabe. I needed to hear that. All of this has made me think about what would have happened to me if I didn't have my uncle," Debbie said, her voice soft in the crisp air.

"And then I think about the people who have nothing. No one to turn to."

Standing a respectful distance away, Gabe watched her with a look of understanding.

"It's tough to be alone this time of year. When it's cold, everyone is supposed to be with family." She wrapped her arms around herself as though feeling the chill of loneliness she described. "I've been thinking... I want to find a way of helping people. Maybe there's a charity or something where I can lend a hand. I'm talking about helping everyone, *Englishers* included. Not just our community."

Gabe's silhouette moved slightly as he stepped closer, his voice warm and encouraging. "I can't believe you're saying that. Just yesterday, I found a place that helps with food and children's toys for the less fortunate."

Debbie's face lit up, the idea taking root in her heart like a seed in fertile soil. "Really?"

"Yes. They do incredible work with people who are struggling."

A sense of purpose surged within Debbie, her posture straightening as if she were ready to embark on this new path at that very moment. "I'd love to help out," she said earnestly.

"I was hoping you'd say that. They're always looking for extra hands. There's something about giving back that makes you feel connected, you know?"

"I've been too involved with myself, my tea business, and focusing on a future with Fritz. I help at community charity events, but I want to do more. This was meant to be."

Gabe's face lit up. "I'm sure it was."

"Do you think I could start tomorrow?" Debbie asked.

Gabe chuckled softly. "Everyone's gathering tomorrow evening. We'll be packing gifts that have been donated for children. Anyone can come. I'll take you there."

"Thanks, Gabe. Oh, but now I have to think about who will look after Jared when I go somewhere. It's so much easier living at Wilma's."

"Bring him with you."

"Are you sure?" she asked.

"Why not? He'll be able to help, too."

Debbie smiled. "I'm sure he'd like that, but I haven't moved yet, so he'll be able to stay here while I'm gone."

The night around them buzzed with the energy of their plans. Debbie's heart swelled with the thought of helping others, of being the beacon of hope that her uncle and Aunt Wilma had been for her.

"Thank you for telling me about this. It feels like I've found a missing piece of myself."

"It's what we're meant to do, Debbie. Give back, help others, and make a difference. We all have our parts to play in making the world a little warmer, a little kinder."

Debbie nodded. "It's the least I can do after all the brightness I've been given."

The conversation continued, the night drawing on,

but the cold was kept at bay by the warmth of their words and the heat of their intentions. They talked of the joy in the children's eyes when they received a gift and the relief in the parents' sighs when they realized they would have a decent meal to share with their family.

As Gabe eventually excused himself to say goodnight to those inside, Debbie lingered on the porch a moment longer. She looked up again at the vast sky, feeling smaller than ever.

She whispered a vow into the night. "I'll be the difference in someone's life." With that, she stepped back into the house, the door closing behind her.

Wilma immediately noticed her entrance and hurried over." Everything okay, Debbie?"

Debbie met her gaze. "I've been thinking, Wilma. I have plans for tomorrow evening, something important I want to do."

Wilma listened intently as Debbie shared her intentions, her expression shifting from worry to admiration.

After hearing Debbie out, Wilma nodded in approval. "That sounds like an excellent idea, Debbie. It'll be good for you. And you say you're going with Gabe?"

"Yes."

Wilma's lips curved upward. "Good. Ada will be pleased."

Debbie frowned. "Will she?"

"Oh yes. She likes Gabe. Now, spend some time

with Mercy and Honor. They leave tomorrow." Wilma took Debbie's arm and led her to where everyone was gathered. Mercy had disappeared into the kitchen with Favor, and they were whispering. Wilma scolded them and told them to come out with the others.

CHAPTER 10

It was early morning when two cars carrying Mercy and Honor's families pulled up in the driveway of Wilma's home.

They spilled out of the car to say their farewells.

Wilma stood at the edge of the porch, her hand lightly resting on the wooden railing, her eyes misty with the sorrow of parting.

Krystal, Cherish, and Favor were also there to say goodbye, along with Debbie and Jared.

The children's laughter and calls punctuated the cool air as Mercy and Honor made their rounds, hugging each woman tightly.

"Call us the moment you have the baby," Mercy told Favor.

"Yes, we want to hear all about it. When the baby's old enough, you'll have to come up and visit us," Honor added.

"I'd like that."

"Do you have names yet, Favor? I can offer some suggestions," Ada said.

"It's fine, thanks. We want to see what the baby looks like first."

Ada shrugged. "Strange, but if that's what you want to do, that's fine."

Mercy brushed away a tear. "I'm sorry we didn't have enough time to sew curtains for you, Debbie. I wish we didn't have to go so soon." Mercy gave everyone another hug and one last one for her mother before walking to the car.

Honor and Mercy's families followed and got into the two waiting cars. Wilma stepped down from the porch, her hand reaching out in a lingering farewell. The cars' engines hummed to life, their soft rumbling breaking the hush that had fallen over the group.

"Safe travels!" Krystal called out, waving vigorously.

A tear trailed down Wilma's cheek as the cars began to pull away. The sight of the taillights receding into the distance felt too final.

Jared ran partway down the driveway, waving at them.

At Wilma's feet, Red, her faithful canine companion, nudged her gently with his nose. His deep brown eyes seemed to understand her sadness as he pressed against her legs.

Wilma bent down to wrap her arms around him, burying her face in his thick fur. "They'll be back, Red," she murmured. "It's not goodbye, just 'till next time."

She stood again, watching until the last car turned at the bend.

"Why don't you visit them soon, *Mamm?*" Cherish suggested.

"No, I can't. Who would look after Red?"

"Take him with you," Favor said.

"Or Jared and I could look after him," Debbie offered as Jared returned to the house.

"Look after who?" Jared asked.

"Red, if Aunt Wilma goes away."

"Yeah. We can do that." He leaned down and hugged Red.

"Thank you. I'll think about it. Maybe Ada will come with me again."

CHAPTER 11

*J*ust after Ada arrived at Wilma's, Daphne and Susan entered for their regular morning tea, joining the women in the cozy living room. Debbie and Krystal had gone to work, and Jared was at school.

Amid the comfort of well-worn armchairs and homely sofas, they each found their spots, sipping hot tea and nibbling on an assortment of leftovers from Debbie's wedding. Since they knew the cakes and treats were from the wedding, the conversation naturally gravitated toward Fritz's hasty exit from town.

Wilma leaned in closer to Daphne and Susan, a slice of cake in her hand. "Did you know that Debbie's planning to move into her own place nearby?"

Daphne reached for another slice of cake. "Really? That's quite a step for Debbie."

Susan, sipping her tea, nodded in agreement. "It's good to see her branching out. How close will she be?"

As the conversation flowed, Cherish set down her cup, the tea barely touched. "Speaking of being busy, I'm concerned about Malachi."

"No one said anything about being busy."

"Oh." Cherish giggled. "I must've been thinking how busy Debbie is. Anyway, I didn't expect to be away this long, and Malachi's got his hands full with our farm, and he's helping Simon and Melvin."

"Are you worried about him?" Wilma asked.

Cherish's fingers traced the rim of her teacup, "In a way. He's been juggling so much lately, and I wish I could be there to help. It's hard because I want to be here too."

The women nodded sympathetically.

Ada, sipping her tea, laughed lightly. "Farmers relish their work from dawn till dusk without a break. He'll be fine, Cherish."

"I know. He'll be able to do it all. He doesn't need breaks; he loves his work," Cherish quickly added.

Savoring a mouthful of chocolate cake, Susan turned the conversation back to the wedding that never was. "You managed to hold it together on the wedding day, Wilma. You made the day a day of fellowship instead of turning the guests away."

Wilma was pleased that someone appreciated what she'd done. "It was hard to know what to do. I just did what I thought was best."

Daphne said, "She couldn't have just told everyone to go home. All the food would've gone to waste."

"I know." Susan took a delicate sip of her tea, the steam fogging her glasses momentarily.

Ada sighed deeply. "Leaving Debbie so unexpectedly... It's a hurt that won't easily fade for Debbie. It'll stay with her forever."

Harriet added, "Time may heal, but some scars stay forever."

"Time heals all wounds," Ada said wistfully. "But time also waits for no man or woman, I suppose."

"The best way she can heal is to get her mind off herself. She's doing something with Gabe involving working for a charity," Wilma said.

Ada swung around to face Wilma. "How do you know that?"

"She told me," Wilma replied, passing Ada a plate of chocolate cupcakes.

Ada took one and placed it on her plate. "And you didn't think to tell me earlier?"

Wilma shrugged, a half-smile on her face. "I guess it slipped my mind."

Favor put her hand on her stomach. "I don't think being around the unfortunate will help her now. It might make her sadder, and she'll feel even more sorry for herself."

"Well, we'll have to wait and see," Harriet said.

Ada pushed out her lips. "I suppose it will keep her mind off herself."

"And she's doing the charity work with Gabe. They're doing it together." Wilma glanced sideways at Ada and saw her lips turn upward at the corners.

CHAPTER 12

That evening, Debbie and Gabe arrived at the charity warehouse, a large, nondescript building on the outskirts of town. As they stepped inside, they were greeted by a hive of activity. Volunteers bustled about, packing donated gifts into boxes to be distributed to needy families.

The air was filled with a sense of purpose as a volunteer coordinator, a tall woman with a clipboard, approached them. "It's good to have you back again, Gabe."

"Thank you. This is my friend, Debbie."

"Welcome, Debbie. We're so glad you're here to help. We've got a lot of gifts to sort through and pack today."

Debbie and Gabe were soon assigned to a station where they began sorting through donations. Toys, books, clothes, and other items were organized into different categories.

"Look at this one," Debbie said, holding up a small stuffed bear with a red bow. "This will make a child very happy."

Gabe smiled. "Yeah, it's amazing how something so simple can bring so much joy."

As they packed the gifts, they chatted with other volunteers, sharing stories and laughter. The atmosphere was joyous; everyone united in the goal of bringing some happiness to others.

A couple of hours later, the coordinator announced a break. Over coffee and snacks, Debbie and Gabe sat down with a group of volunteers. Conversations flowed easily, and Debbie opened up about her recent challenges.

"It's been a tough year," she admitted. "But being here, doing this, it helps put things in perspective."

An older man with kind eyes nodded in agreement. "Giving to others has a way of healing us, too. It's one of life's circles."

As the evening progressed, the warehouse transformed from a clutter of donations to neatly packed boxes, each waiting to be delivered.

At the end of the night, the coordinator gathered everyone together. "Thanks to your hard work, hundreds of families will have a brighter winter season. You've all made a huge difference."

Debbie felt a sense of fulfilment. She had come to help others, but in return, she had received much more in the simple act of giving.

As they left the warehouse, Gabe turned to Debbie. "Today was a good day."

Debbie nodded. "Thank you for telling me about this."

They walked to the horse and buggy, their steps light, their hearts full. Debbie realized that she'd spent the whole evening having a good time and, best of all, she hadn't thought about Fritz once.

CHAPTER 13

The day of the horse auction finally arrived. Samuel, Eli, and Debbie sat together on Wilma's porch, their eyes fixed on the road, waiting for the horse expert that Ada had arranged to accompany them.

The morning air was filled with the promise of new beginnings, and the sound of nature was punctuated by the occasional clop of horse hooves in the distance. They expected to see a horse and buggy appear at any moment, signaling the arrival of the expert.

However, their attention was diverted by an unexpected arrival. They saw Gabe walking to the house through the apple orchard.

As Gabe reached the porch, he stopped and placed his hands on his hips, casting a curious glance at the trio. "We're all going to the auction?" he asked, a smile playing on his lips.

Debbie responded, "Yes, we are waiting for the

horse expert Ada recommended. We didn't know you were interested in coming along."

"She suggested I come along too. I hope you don't mind."

"I'm glad you've got the time," Debbie said.

Gabe sat down on the porch steps and waited along with them.

Eli, always practical, chimed in, "It's going to be a busy day. Lots of horses to see and decisions to make."

Samuel, nodding in agreement, added, "It's good to have more eyes and opinions. It's an important decision for Debbie."

Just as their conversation was meandering through various topics, the door behind them creaked open. Ada poked her head out. "Well, what are you all waiting for?" she inquired.

Samuel replied, "We're waiting for this horse expert you mentioned, dear."

Ada's brow furrowed as she looked at her husband and then at Gabe. "You've been waiting for Gabe, and now he's here. There's no one else coming."

Debbie, looking slightly embarrassed, turned to Gabe. "Oh, we didn't know. Sorry, Gabe," she said. The revelation seemed to add a new layer of surprise to the morning's proceedings.

Samuel stared at Gabe. "We didn't know you were a horse expert."

Gabe shrugged. "Neither did I."

Ada chuckled lightly. "I don't think I said 'expert.' He knows about horses, don't you, Gabe?"

Gabe, with a modest shrug, responded, "I do, but I'm not sure I know more than anyone else."

Debbie's face lit up with a grateful smile. "Well, you certainly know more than me, I'm sure," she said enthusiastically. "So, let's go."

"Bye now," Ada said waving at them. Then Ada closed the door and looked over at Wilma who was standing behind the door.

The pair of them burst out laughing. "Oh, Ada, you're so funny. Your plan worked, but it nearly didn't. Do you really think Debbie and Gabe could fall in love?"

"Hmm. The only fly in the ointment is Jared. He's a handful. Would Gabe be up for the challenge?"

Wilma thought for a moment. "I think he would." Then, they raced to the living room window and looked out.

They were in time to see Debbie get into the buggy. She sat beside Gabe while Samuel drove, and Eli sat beside him. The rhythmic clip-clopping of the horse's hooves provided a soothing soundtrack to their expedition.

Debbie's eyes sparkled with a mix of nervousness and excitement. It wasn't every day that one got to choose a horse.

CHAPTER 14

Gabe, sensing her unease, turned to her with a smile. "What are you looking for in a horse, Debbie?"

Debbie thought for a moment, her gaze drifting over the passing fields. "Well, I'd like one with a good temperament," she began tentatively. "Something reliable and gentle. And young, but not too young."

"A good temperament is essential."

Focusing on the road, Eli said, "You'll want a horse that's easy to train, responsive, but not overly spirited. A young one has its advantages, but too young, and you might find yourself with more than you bargained for."

"A lot of buggy horses are Standardbreds. They make excellent buggy horses," Samuel said.

Debbie's interest was piqued. "Standardbred? I don't know much about them."

"They're usually calm and intelligent."

Eli nodded in agreement. "He's right. They're sturdy

and have a steady disposition. Plus, they're generally easier to train than some more high-spirited breeds."

The conversation turned to tales of horses they had known, with each sharing experiences and anecdotes. Eli recalled a Standardbred he had once worked with, praising its quick learning ability and even temperament. Gabe shared stories from the horse auctions he had attended, highlighting the qualities of different breeds he had encountered.

As the group arrived at the bustling horse auction, the air was electric with the energy of prospective buyers and sellers, horses' sounds, and the crowd's lively chatter.

Samuel and Eli, well-known figures in their Amish community, were quickly drawn into conversations with friends, leaving Debbie and Gabe alone.

"It looks like it's just us," Gabe quipped.

"That's fine. Let's go look at the horses."

They ventured towards the rows of horses that were to be auctioned. Debbie's gaze moved from one horse to another.

Gabe said, "I was impressed with how you handled everything at the charity the other night."

Debbie smiled up at him. "Thanks, Gabe. It was a bit chaotic, but I enjoyed it."

"Remember, we're doing it again next week. You'll be there, right?"

Debbie's face lit up with enthusiasm. "I wouldn't miss it. It feels good to be involved, to do something meaningful."

As they continued along the row of horses, their conversation flowed effortlessly. They discussed the various qualities of the horses they saw, with Debbie pointing out those she found appealing based on the advice she had received earlier.

The crowd swelled around the auctioneer's stand as the auction time neared. Samuel and Eli, having finished their conversations, re-joined Debbie and Gabe.

"There's a horse I saw earlier that I liked. Gabe likes it too," Debbie told them.

"Oh? Tell us about it," Eli said.

Debbie's smile widened. "Well, it has a gentle demeanor, just the right temperament. It's young but not too inexperienced," she explained. "It seemed calm but alert, exactly the kind of horse I could connect with."

Gabe added, "It's a Standardbred, about five years old. It's been trained under harness, too."

Samuel, impressed, turned to Debbie. "He sounds good, so let's hope we can get him at a reasonable price."

As the auctioneer began calling attention to the start of the auction, the group's conversation drew to a close. They positioned themselves where they had a good view of the horses.

Debbie's anticipation peaked when the horse she had her eye on was finally brought out. The horse looked even more impressive. Its coat shined in the sun, and his head was held high as he was led around the ring.

With the support of Eli, Samuel, and Gabe, Debbie raised her hand to place a bid. The bidding was nerve-wracking, with several other interested parties driving the price up. But Debbie stayed in the bidding, determined to secure the horse she had set her heart on.

Finally, after a few tense minutes, the auctioneer called out, "Sold!"

Debbie's bid was the winner.

A wave of relief washed over her, and she turned to her friends, her face beaming with happiness. "Thank you, everyone. I couldn't have done this without your help."

"Now we have to get him home," Eli said.

"And you have to pay them," Samuel added.

"This way." Eli strode toward the office and Debbie quickly followed.

After the payment, the arrangements were made for the horse to be trucked to Wilma's house.

On the way home, Debbie said, "Now all I need is a buggy."

"Would you mind an older one?" Eli asked.

"I don't mind at all as long as it's a safe one. Do you know of one for sale?"

"I do, and it would suit your pocket. It's free. I've got one I'm not using," he said. "I have three, and this one was Frannie's."

Debbie's heart skipped a beat at the mention of Eli's late wife. She knew how fondly Eli spoke of Frannie, and she couldn't help but feel a wave of hesitation. "Oh, I couldn't take it."

Eli turned around and grinned at her. "Frannie would have wanted her buggy to be helpful rather than just sitting in the barn gathering dust. I believe in making good use of things and not letting things go to waste. The buggy is in good condition, and I'd rather it help someone who needs it. I can't think of a better person to use it than you."

Samuel nodded in agreement. "Eli's right, Debbie. It's a kind gesture, and you accepting it would give the buggy a new lease on life."

"That's right. It's what Frannie would have wanted," Eli said.

"It sounds like a generous offer," Gabe said.

The warmth and sincerity in their voices helped ease Debbie's initial apprehension. She looked at Eli, the kindness in his eyes reassuring her. "If you're sure, Eli, I'd be honored to use it. I promise to take good care of it."

Eli's face lit up with a smile. "I am sure. And I know you will."

.

CHAPTER 15

While Debbie was busy at the horse auction, Wilma dipped her brush into the blue paint. She glanced around Jared's new room. He wanted a blue room, and this room was becoming blue fast.

Because Harriet was detail-oriented, she had been given the job of painting the edges while Ada was painting the opposite wall.

Hearing laughter from the kitchen, Wilma poked her head around the doorway. She was shocked to see how bright the yellow was on the walls.

"Careful with that paint, Cherish!" Wilma called out, chuckling as Cherish narrowly avoided a paint spill. "We want the kitchen to look sunny, not like a crime scene."

Cherish rolled her eyes playfully. "I'll have you know, I'm an artist with this brush."

Wilma smiled. "That would be a true miracle."

"It's all right, *Mamm*. I'm watching her," Hope said.

"Oh, Wilma, would you mind checking on Favor?" Harriet asked.

"Sure."

Wilma took a few more steps and saw Favor wrapped in a blanket, watching them through the window.

"She really should be helping," Hope muttered, not unkindly, from the kitchen. "But I guess being pregnant has its perks."

Overhearing the comment, Harriet set her brush down and walked into the kitchen. "Let her be," she said gently. "Pregnancy isn't always easy. She's doing what's best for her and the baby."

"I think it's time for a break, Wilma. I'll use up the last of the paint on this brush."

"I like the sound of that," Wilma said as she walked to the kitchen table. Ada and Wilma had brought everything with them for a picnic lunch.

She began unpacking sandwiches and fruit, arranging them neatly.

Hope helped Wilma set out the food on the blanket on the floor while Bliss boiled water on the gas stove for tea.

"This is perfect," Bliss said, her voice content. "There's nothing like a good cup of hot tea to break up a day of hard work."

"I agree. It's always time for tea," Ada said.

They all sat down on the floor to eat. The younger women sat cross-legged while the older ladies tried different positions before becoming comfortable. Favor sat slightly behind them in the only chair in the house.

"Debbie's going to love what we've done with the place," Hope said, biting into a tomato and cheese sandwich.

Wilma nodded, her heart warm with the thought of their friend's reaction. "She deserves this fresh start," she said, "and we're going to make sure she gets it."

"Jah, fresh paint for a fresh start," Ada added with a laugh. Then Ada's attention turned to Hope. "So, Hope, are you any closer to starting a family soon?"

Hope stopped chewing her mouthful and hung her head.

A flicker of realization crossed Ada's face. "Oh, I'm sorry. I remember you asked us not to keep bringing that up."

Hope gave a small, understanding smile. "It's alright, Ada. I guess people just want to know. If and when I have any news, I won't be keeping it to myself."

Wilma watched the exchange, feeling empathy for her daughter Hope. She knew the question was a sensitive one. It had to be hard watching her sisters have babies.

"Jah, I'll tell everyone too if I have baby news," Cherish said.

"Me as well. I don't have any babies yet, as you all know. I'm trying to understand why. All we can do is pray. We can pray for each other," Bliss suggested.

"A prayer circle. What a good idea," Harriet said. "I

know what you girls are going through. I lost many babies before I had Simon. It was a long road, but I was blessed with one son, and now God has given me a daughter." She smiled at Favor, who was not looking very happy.

"What's wrong, Favor?" Wilma asked.

"I'm not comfortable."

"None of us are," Ada said. "Would you like to try the floor?"

"No. I wouldn't be able to get up. I'm just hoping I'll be able to get out of this chair."

Everyone laughed.

"We'll pull you out if we need to," Cherish said.

"Has anyone given any thought to furniture for the house? Does Debbie have any?" Hope asked.

"I saw some up in the attic, but when I had a better look it's not so good. She'll need two beds, a couch, and a table and chairs," Harriet said.

"Why don't you ask Carter to buy things for her, Wilma?" Ada suggested.

Wilma's mouth opened in shock. "I can't do that."

Ada shrugged her shoulders. "Why? He has loads of money. More than he needs."

"Well, we can't ask him to do that. He's already generous enough with us." Wilma couldn't think of anything worse. Carter would feel used.

"When we finish the painting, why don't we put our heads together and go out and get some furniture for this place?" Cherish suggested.

"Who would pay for it?" Bliss asked.

Cherish shrugged. "We'll figure it out. We can all pitch in a bit, and maybe we can find some good deals. It doesn't have to be extravagant, just something to make the house feel like a home."

The idea lit up the room.

"I love that idea, Cherish," Harriet exclaimed. "We can make it a fun outing, searching for beautiful, affordable pieces that fit perfectly in each room."

Hope nodded enthusiastically. "And we can put our creativity to use. I love doing things like that. We can find unique pieces that reflect Debbie's personality and make her feel at home."

Ada chimed in. "I know a few local furniture shops that offer great deals. We can start there and see what catches our eye. And if we need more funds, I'm sure we can reach out to the community for support."

"Okay, ladies. We need to hurry with the painting. I'd like to have some furniture in by the end of the day," Wilma announced. "We'll give Debbie a real surprise."

"It seems a hard task, Wilma. Almost an impossible one. But I heard a saying I like. Where there is a will, there is a way."

Wilma chuckled. "You and your sayings, Ada."

~

Wilma clapped her hands as the last brushstroke was laid, drawing everyone's attention. "Alright, team, it's time for our next job furnishing this home."

Ada, wiping paint from her hands, grinned. "I'm in.

But where do we start? Debbie's house is as bare as a newborn."

Harriet, meticulously cleaning her brushes, added, "We'll need the basics. Beds, a sofa, dining table... Let's make a list."

Cherish chimed in. "I saw a new thrift store the other day. We might find some things there."

Bliss, pouring the last of the tea, suggested, "Why not split up? Cover more ground that way. Some of us can hit the thrift stores; others can check out sales at furniture shops."

Hope, looking thoughtful, said, "We also need to consider the budget. We can't go overboard."

Wilma nodded. "Agreed. We'll each contribute what we can. Every little bit helps."

Ada added, "And let's not forget about asking around. Sometimes people have things they're looking to give away."

As they mapped out their plan, Favor spoke up hesitantly from her chair, "I wish I could help more..."

Harriet immediately reassured her. "You're doing plenty, Favor. Just take care of yourself and the little one."

"I'll clean up after you're gone. Leave the brushes and everything. I'll have it done before you get back," Favor said. "I want to contribute something."

"Very well. As long as you're up to it," Wilma said.

"I can do it."

The group split into teams, each with a specific task. Ada, Harriet, and Bliss headed to the thrift store, while Wilma, Cherish, and Hope decided to explore the furniture shops.

At the thrift store, Ada's keen eye spotted a slightly worn sofa. "Look at this! It's perfect for the living room, and with a little cleaning, it will be as good as new."

Bliss, examining a set of curtains, agreed. "What you can find here is amazing. These curtains would add such a nice touch to the living room."

Meanwhile, Wilma, Cherish, and Hope were at a furniture shop, discussing a dining table. Cherish saw the potential. "This table will be stunning with a fresh coat of paint."

Hope, checking their budget, nodded. "It's a great find. Let's get it. There will be no time to paint it today, though."

"Yeah. Well, that can be done later."

After buying the table, they persuaded the store's owner to have it delivered immediately. The owner agreed, and then they spotted two beds on sale. The owner threw them in, too, for a good discount.

As the day wore on, they reconvened at Debbie's house, each team bearing their treasures. The house slowly came to life as they arranged the furniture that was miraculously delivered the same day.

Wilma, stepping back to admire their work, said, "Debbie's going to be so surprised. This place is completely transformed."

Harriet, placing the last cushion on the sofa, smiled. "It's more than a house now. It's a home."

"It was meant to be that we found all these things. I hope Debbie likes what we chose." Ada bit her lip as she looked around.

"She will love it all," Bliss said.

Hope looked around at everyone. "We did it. We made something beautiful together."

"And now we have to get home. Debbie will soon be coming home from the horse auction," Wilma said as she shooed everyone out the door.

~

When Debbie and the others returned to Wilma's house from the horse auction, Wilma and Ada hurried out to hear the news.

When they all left the buggy, Samuel said, "We got a horse."

"When do we see it?" Wilma asked.

Everyone looked at Debbie. "It's being trucked here tomorrow."

"So, you got a good one?" Ada asked, stepping closer.

Debbie nodded. "I did. I couldn't have chosen one without everyone's help."

Gabe, standing a bit to the side, smiled warmly. "I should go now. I'll see you all later."

"I'll go too. Bye now."

Debbie turned to them. "Thank you so much for helping. It's really been a great day."

Once Gabe and Eli were gone, Wilma clapped her

hands together. "Well, this calls for a celebration! We should have a proper introduction for the new member of your family, Debbie."

Ada nodded in agreement. "Absolutely! We can all come together tomorrow to see the horse. What do you think, Debbie?"

"That sounds wonderful. I'd love that," Debbie said. "And Eli offered me a buggy. Now I'm all set. I'll be independent. It's Frannie's old buggy and he insisted I take it. I didn't know what to say, but he urged me to say I'd have it."

As they chatted excitedly about the next day's plans, the group slowly entered Wilma's house.

Harriet stared at Wilma. "Are you going to tell Debbie anything?"

Wilma grinned at Debbie. "We need to show you what we did today. We've finished."

"You finished the painting already?" Debbie asked.

"Let's take you over and have a quick look at it now before we start cooking the evening meal. Favor can stay and look after Jared," Wilma suggested.

"Sure. I'll do that. Um. Does anyone know where he is?" Favor asked looking around.

"He'll be outside. Probably with the horses or out the back looking at birds. He never stays out late," Debbie assured her.

CHAPTER 16

*D*ebbie stepped tentatively into her house, her eyes wide with anticipation. Her hands flew to her mouth when she saw the transformation, and tears welled in her eyes.

She walked slowly through the house, taking it all in. The once-empty rooms were now filled with color, warmth, and life. Every corner held a touch of her friends' love and effort.

The living room, with its cozy sofa and vibrant curtains, beckoned her to sit and relax. The dining area with a sturdy table promised future gatherings and laughter. Her bedroom also featured a new bed and someone had found the quilt that Krystal had given her and placed it on top.

When they moved to Jared's room, she saw the walls were already blue and there was also a bed.

Wilma looked over Debbie's shoulder. "We didn't have time to get sheets. But we'll do that."

"Oh no. I can do it." Overwhelmed, Debbie turned to her friends, her voice trembling. "I... I can't believe you did all this. For me."

Wilma stepped forward, her own eyes glistening. "You've always been there for us, Debbie. It was our turn to be there for you."

Harriet, with a gentle smile, added, "We wanted to give you a fresh start, a place that feels like home."

Cherish, bouncing excitedly, said, "And we had so much fun doing it. Even Favor helped."

"I hope she didn't get worn out. I love the bright kitchen. It's perfect. It's all just perfect."

Hope said warmly, "We're just glad we could help, Debbie. You deserve this and so much more."

Debbie took a deep breath, looking around at the faces of her friends, each beaming with joy and satisfaction. "I don't know how to thank you all. You've turned this house into a home. You've given me more than just furniture and paint; you've reminded me of the incredible friends and family I have."

Before they left for Wilma's house, they sat and chatted for a while.

Debbie, looked around. "This is more than I could have ever asked for. You all have worked so hard. I can't wait to make new memories here with all of you. I can't wait to move in."

A FEW DAYS LATER, the time came for Ruth, Favor, Cherish, and Harriet to depart. The air was filled with the bittersweet tang of farewells and promises to stay connected.

Krystal had left for work, and Debbie and Wilma stood on the porch.

Harriet and Cherish were busy loading the suitcases into Ruth's car.

"Remember to keep me updated on your pregnancy, Favor," Wilma called out.

Favor smiled and nodded with a hand resting gently on her belly. "Of course, *Mamm*. I'll call you with every little update."

Harriet, who had been quietly helping with the bags, said, "Don't you worry, Wilma. She'll be in good hands. I won't leave her side."

Wilma's eyes softened as she looked at Harriet, grateful for her reassuring presence. "Thank you, Harriet. I know she will be."

Cherish came up to hug her mother. "We'll miss you, *Mamm*. But we'll be back before you know it, or you can visit us."

Wilma hugged her tightly. "I hope that's true. Safe travels, and remember, you're always welcome home."

Debbie hugged everyone goodbye, and the group gathered for a final farewell.

Ruth revved the car's engine playfully. "Alright, ladies, time to hit the road. Let's make this a trip to remember."

Wilma watched as they piled into the car, a lively

tangle of hugs, laughter, and last-minute reminders. As the car pulled away, Wilma stepped into the middle of the driveway and waved.

The car stopped near the road, and Wilma noticed Ada and Samuel's buggy turning into the driveway. Ada and Samuel got out and went to each window, saying goodbye. Then Samuel got back in the horse and buggy and moved away. The car moved on, and Ada was left to walk up the long driveway.

Debbie waved hello to Ada and then told Wilma she'd be up in her room packing.

Ada finally reached the porch.

"Your foot must have fully recovered," Wilma said.

"Don't worry about my foot. Are you alright?"

Wilma nodded as she held back tears. "I'm okay. It was good to see them. Seeing them go is sad, but I'm glad they came."

Ada moved forward and patted Wilma's shoulder. "Why don't we visit them as soon as Favor's baby is born?"

"I think I will. Will you come with me?"

"Always. Now, how about a hot cup of tea?" Ada asked.

They both moved into the house.

As they sat sipping their cups of tea, Wilma said, "It's going to be so much quieter with all of them gone. Now it's just me, Red, and Krystal living here."

Ada chuckled. "I like how you mention the dog."

Wilma looked at Red, stretched out and asleep on the floor. "He's good company."

"Jah, when he's awake, which isn't much." Ada chuckled again. "Wilma, it'll take a while to get used to Debbie living away from here, but life is constantly changing."

"It seems that just as I get used to things, they change, and I must adapt. But things never change for you, Ada. Why is that?"

Ada paused, considering Wilma's observation. She set her cup of tea down. "Well, Wilma, it's not that things don't change for me. It's more that I've learned to ride the waves of change rather than fighting against them."

Wilma looked thoughtful. "Maybe."

Ada leaned back in her chair, her gaze drifting towards the window. "Life's too short to stay anchored in one spot, Wilma. Change is inevitable, but it also brings new opportunities, new experiences."

"Unwelcome or not. Debbie wouldn't have chosen what Fritz did. That's not a good change for her."

"Well, I think she'll look back in a year or two and realize that it was the best thing for her."

Wilma nodded, her mind wandering to the recent changes in her life. "You know, sometimes I wish things could stay the same. I like staying with the comfortable, the familiar. But then I see that Debbie and Fritz might not have been happy, so you're probably right about that."

Ada smiled warmly. "Exactly. We were right about him at the start. We found him arrogant, do you remember?"

"I do, but then I forgave his attitude and thought he might have been in a bad mood."

"You're such a forgiving person, and that's a good thing. There's something I've been meaning to ask."

Wilma looked up. "Yes?"

"Do you ever think about Obadiah?"

Wilma's eyebrows shot up. "Certainly not. He didn't even come for Debbie's wedding. It shows he doesn't care about me at all. If he cared, he'd care about my family."

Ada searched Wilma's face for a moment. "He could be ill or have a good reason. You won't know until you talk with him. I know you had something special going on with him."

"Ada, I've made my decision. Could you please stop mentioning his name?"

CHAPTER 17

Ada frowned at Wilma's reaction, which was more of an outburst. "I've barely mentioned his name since you decided you didn't need a third husband." Ada chuckled at her own words. "Oh, I didn't mean that you would've had three all at once. I'm pleased no one can hear us right now. They might've got the wrong idea."

Wilma wasn't smiling, so Ada shifted in her seat, and the conversation moved to memories of their youth, the changes they had witnessed and experienced over the years. They reminisced about the days when their children were small, the challenges they faced, and the joyous moments that filled their hearts.

As the afternoon wore on, the comfort of their shared memories and the warmth of the tea soothed Wilma's initial sadness.

"Thanks for being here," Wilma said sincerely. "I don't know what I'd do without you."

SAMANTHA PRICE

Ada reached across the table, giving Wilma's hand a reassuring squeeze. "That's what friends are for. We're here to lift each other up."

"I wish there was more we could do for Debbie."

"Maybe there is."

Wilma stared at Ada's smiling face. "What are you thinking?"

"Why don't we take over her tea stall for a couple of weeks? It'll allow her to settle into her new home and routine."

Wilma thought about it for a moment. "Will she allow us?"

"Of course, she would. Why wouldn't she?"

"How do you know she will?" Wilma inquired.

"Debbie!" Ada called out at the top of her lungs.

Wilma jumped with fright over Ada's sudden yell. After a moment, a breathless Debbie ran into the kitchen. "What's going on?" Debbie asked.

"Wilma and I want to take over your tea stall for a couple of weeks. You know, give you a break," Ada said, grinning.

"We'll run it for you," Wilma added.

Debbie's eyes widened. "Oh. I thought something bad had happened when you called out so loud, Ada."

"No. I just wanted you to hear me. Nothing's wrong. Now, what do you say about our idea?"

Debbie stared at Ada for a moment before breaking into a wide smile. "Really? You two would do that?"

"Of course we would. We've been thinking of what we can do to help out. We don't have our little shop open at this time of year, so we have plenty of time on our hands."

Debbie's eyes misted. "You don't know how much this means to me. I'd love it. Bliss has been there for me, but she needs a break too."

"Don't mention it. We'll start tomorrow. Tell us what we need to know, and we'll take it from there."

Debbie threw her arms around Ada and Wilma, hugging them tightly. "This will give me time to make the house a proper home for Jared. I'll come with you in the morning and show you the ropes. Then I'll come back at closing time."

As Debbie continued talking, Wilma's mind drifted to Obadiah. The whole thing with Fritz had reminded Wilma how precious and rare true love was. She had special feelings for Obadiah, but the fear of losing another husband was real.

Then she reminded herself once again that Obadiah hadn't even bothered to contact her since she'd asked him to leave and told him she wasn't interested. He wouldn't have given up so quickly if he had really loved her.

wanted to raise Jared? If anyone can turn a bad situation around, it's her."

Harriet let out a giant yawn and covered her mouth. "Ah, excuse me."

"Well, I don't know about all of you, but I'll be pleased to get home," Cherish said. "I feel like I haven't seen Malachi for weeks."

"Harriet, do you think they would've finished building onto the house yet?" Favor asked.

"I hope so. Then we can get things set up for when our baby arrives."

Cherish was surprised to hear Harriet call Favor's baby 'our' baby, but Favor didn't seem to mind.

CHAPTER 19

Hours later, Favor stepped out of Ruth's car into the crisp air, a hand resting gently on her swelling belly. Harriet got out, too, and her gaze lingered on the newly built extension of the family home.

"Look, Favor, it's finally complete. Well, it certainly looks it from here." Harriet's eyes were wide with wonder.

"They've done a lot since we've been gone," Cherish said.

"Let's have a closer look." Harriet led the way. Ruth got out of the car and followed.

The extension, a robust wood and stone structure, stood proudly against the backdrop of Favor and Simon's non-traditional Amish home.

They walked to the doorway and looked at the small living room with the kitchen in one corner.

Favor moved slowly, her hand caressing the smooth

surfaces of the kitchen cupboards, imagining the laughter and love the room would soon contain. "It's more than I ever hoped for. Now, we can all be together, but not together, Harriet."

"Ma," Harriet gently reminded Favor.

"Ma." Favor repeated with a grin.

Cherish stayed silent, still shocked that Favor would want her meddling in-laws so close. She'd never get used to how Favor had quickly changed her mind about Harriet and Melvin.

As they admired the new addition, Simon and Melvin emerged from the main house, their faces beaming.

"Welcome home, my love," Simon said, putting his arm around Favor.

Melvin nodded at Harriet and the others with a satisfied grin.

"We wanted to surprise you," Simon continued, guiding Favor through his parents' new space. "Pa and I, along with some help from the community, worked hard to get this done as quickly as we could. What do you think of it, Ma?"

Harriet looked around. "It's perfect. Thank you."

Favor looked around, her eyes taking in every detail. "It's beautiful," she murmured.

Melvin added, "There's still some interior work to be done in the bedrooms, but we'll have it ready well before the baby arrives."

Harriet nodded her approval, a rare smile touching her lips.

"We'll finish it within a couple of weeks, I'd say," Simon said.

The women wandered through the two bedrooms and the small bathroom, discussing plans for furnishings.

As they talked, Favor imagined a crib in the corner of one of the bedrooms for when Harriet had the baby overnight. Her mother had been somewhat distant and distracted when she'd been growing up. That's why it was nice to have Harriet solely focused on her and her baby.

Ruth nodded. "It all looks good, a great addition to the neighborhood. And where are the alpacas?"

Melvin pointed in the distance. "They're in that yard. We've got more coming."

"Ah, good. You've got the place nicely set up for an extended family farm. So, Cherish, are you ready to go?" Ruth asked.

"Yes, I'm ready."

They said their goodbyes, and then Cherish and Ruth returned to the car.

Ruth's car rolled to a stop in front of Cherish's house a few minutes later. The silence was suddenly broken by the sound of excited barking from Caramel. Malachi came out of the barn and hurried to the car with Wally, the goose, following behind.

Malachi's face lit up with a joyous smile as he helped Cherish out. His arms enveloped her in a warm embrace while Wally and Caramel swirled around their feet.

SAMANTHA PRICE

Ruth watched from the driver's seat, a chuckle escaping as she witnessed the scene. "I wish I had someone to welcome me like that," she said, laughing.

Ruth rolled down the window and said, "You two never get tired of each other!"

"Never," Cherish said as she leaned down to pat Caramel.

"How was the wedding?" Malachi asked them.

Cherish and Ruth looked at each other. Then Cherish told him, "The wedding never happened."

He frowned. "What do you mean?"

Cherish shook her head. "It's a long story. Oh, I need to get my things, Ruth."

Ruth got out of the car and opened the trunk, and Malachi moved to get Cherish's suitcase. "We met Gabe your older brother," Ruth announced.

Malachi's eyebrows shot up in surprise. "Gabe? What was he doing there?"

"Checking up on Jed," Ruth replied. "He said the family sent him to find out when he'd be going home."

"He's fallen in love with Krystal, so he'll never go home. But it seems that Gabe isn't keen to rush home either," Cherish said.

Malachi nodded. "That's not surprising."

Changing the subject, Cherish asked Ruth, "You must be hungry after the long day. Why don't you come in for a meal?"

Ruth shook her head. "Thank you, but I'm quite tired. I'll head straight home."

"Sure, Ruth. But do let us know if you need anything, alright?"

"Will do. You two take care," she said as she returned to the car.

Cherish leaned down, patted Caramel again, and then tried to pat Wally, but he moved away. She stood up straight, and Malachi took her hand and grabbed her suitcase with his other hand. Together, they walked into the house as Ruth's car zoomed away.

Malachi put the suitcase down and then asked about the wedding.

Cherish sighed and sat on the sofa, with Caramel jumping next to her. She told him the whole wedding saga in detail.

Malachi let out a low whistle. "Wow. That was unexpected, wasn't it?"

"It was."

"How is Debbie now?"

"She's heartbroken, of course. She loved Fritz, and she was so excited to marry him. And now, who knows what will happen? Will he come back? Will she move on?" She shook her head. "It's just an embarrassing mess for Debbie. It's not good for Jared either."

Malachi nodded. "Well, maybe this is a blessing in disguise. Fritz isn't the right guy for her after all."

Cherish smiled weakly. "Maybe."

"Maybe?"

"Yes, I mean, of course, he isn't. Even Debbie realizes that now."

SAMANTHA PRICE

Malachi took her hand. "Come on, let's eat. It'll make you feel better. I cooked it myself."

"Really? Toasted sandwiches again?"

Malachi chuckled. "Hey, toasted sandwiches are okay. You can never go wrong with them."

Cherish laughed and got up. "Alright, you've convinced me. Let's eat. I'm so hungry I'll even enjoy your toasted delights."

He laughed. "That's not nice."

They made their way to the kitchen, where Malachi had set the table with a red and white checked tablecloth and a vase of fresh flowers in the center. The aroma of spaghetti sauce filled the air, making Cherish's mouth water.

"It smells like spaghetti and garlic."

"You'll know in a minute." He produced spaghetti with meatballs with garlic bread on the side.

Cherish stared at everything. "This is amazing."

He sat opposite her and grinned. "You're amazing."

She smiled at him, and then they closed their eyes for a silent prayer of thanks.

When they were finished, Cherish looked at Malachi. "I'm grateful for you. Without you, I don't know where I'd be."

"I'm grateful for you too. You make my life better every day."

Cherish reached across the table and took his hand in hers. "You're the best thing that's ever happened to me."

Malachi leaned in. "I love you more than anything. I

hope you don't go anywhere again soon. I missed you too much."

"I missed you as well." Their lips met in a slow, sweet pre-dinner kiss. The pets sat nearby, watching closely.

CHAPTER 20

The morning at Debbie's market stall ambled by at a pace that would make a snail look speedy. Ada tried rearranging the tea packets for the fifth time, hoping a new formation might somehow attract customers. "Maybe if we arrange them in the shape of a heart, it'll draw in the romantics," she suggested with a hopeful grin.

Wilma raised an eyebrow. "Because nothing says romance like a broken engagement and mint tea?"

"I'm trying, Wilma. I don't want Debbie to ask what we sold today, and we tell her we didn't make one cent."

Wilma pressed her lips together. "No. That wouldn't be good. I'll say some prayers."

"I'll say double. But prayers also require action, so we must do something."

"I know."

By lunchtime, no sale had been made, and they started to worry some more.

SAMANTHA PRICE

"Perhaps we should start a new trend—invisible tea," Ada mused, trying to lighten the mood. "It's very exclusive. So exclusive that you can't see or taste it."

Wilma nodded. "Yes, and we'll market it as the perfect drink for avoiding awkward conversations about runaway grooms."

"Or we could start a rumor that drinking our tea makes you irresistibly attractive to men. We'd have a line of women around the block."

Wilma looked up and saw two ladies they knew from the community. "Smile, Ada. We have some likely victims coming our way."

"I hope they need tea, Wilma."

Wilma's mouth turned down at the corners. "Oh, they're going the other way. They didn't see us."

"I can't let them escape! I'll get them." Ada hurried off and, a couple of minutes later, returned with Millie and Kate from their community.

"You're here too, Wilma," Millie said.

"Yes. We're helping out poor Debbie."

Ada nodded. "Yes, and we don't just mean poor because the man left her. She's going to struggle with raising her young boy. You know this is Debbie's tea stall, right?"

Millie nodded. "I have bought tea from her before. She makes wonderful blends."

Ada exchanged a smile with Wilma.

"I could use some tea," Kate said, picking up a packet to read.

"Perfect. I think it's time to stock up." Ada turned around and reached for the rose, white tea. "This is my favorite."

"I'll take two of those and…" Millie leaned forward, examining the selection. "What's that one there?" she asked, pointing at a fragrant blend of chamomile and lavender.

"That's our 'Relaxation Blend,'" Ada replied, her sales pitch gaining momentum. "It's perfect for those evenings when you just want to unwind and forget about all the day's troubles."

"Debbie could certainly use that tea right now," Wilma said, shaking her head.

"I feel so bad for Debbie," Kate mumbled. "Give me two of the relaxation blend."

Ada nodded. "Two it is, and then did you want two of the rose as well? Did you know he has not even tried to contact Debbie? Only left a note, and the note barely said anything."

"A note that broke her heart and shattered her dreams," Wilma added.

"That's dreadful. Make it three of each, Ada. And I'll have three of the licorice tea. Bert likes licorice, so he might enjoy it in tea as well."

"Certainly." Ada carefully placed the tea packets into a large bag. "Did you mean three of every single flavor, Millie?"

Millie bit her lip. "Why not?"

"I'll take the same as Millie," Kate nodded.

SAMANTHA PRICE

Millie, not to be outdone, chimed in, "Throw in an extra of the mint tea as well. And do you have anything for getting rid of unwanted suitors? I have an *Englisher* neighbor who just won't take a hint."

Ada laughed. "I'm afraid Debbie's tea hasn't quite mastered that yet."

"She'll need to work on a tea for attracting suitors first," Wilma said, bringing the conversation back to Debbie's plight.

As they wrapped up the two huge sales, more people began to trickle over, drawn by the laughter and chatter. Ada and Wilma exchanged a relieved glance as the third large order was placed.

After four more sales were made, Nellie Schmidt arrived. "Hello, Ada and Wilma. It's such a shame about Debbie's wedding. How is she holding up?"

Seizing the opportunity, Ada replied with a somber tone, "She's been better, Nellie. We're just here trying to keep her tea stall running. It's been tough for her, especially with her little boy."

Nellie tsked sympathetically. "Well, I must help. Let me buy some of that peppermint tea. It's Abe's favorite."

As Nellie made her purchase, even more people began to stop by. Each expressed their sympathy for Debbie's plight and left with at least one shopping bag full of tea. Ada and Wilma found themselves sharing Debbie's story more times than they could count, and with each telling, they noticed their stock of tea dwindling.

Ned Jacobs, the local baker, stopped by next. "Heard

HER HOPEFUL HEART

about Debbie," he said, shaking his head. "I'll take some of that chai. Might as well stock up for the bakery."

Ada smiled. "That's very kind of you, Mr. Jacobs. Debbie will appreciate it. There are twelve packets here. Will that be enough?"

He gave a nod. "That'll do it."

By mid-afternoon, the stall had become the center of the market's attention. People who had never heard of Debbie were keen to support her. Nearly every sale was helped along by Ada and Wilma's stories about the young woman who'd been deserted by the man she had loved.

Usually more reserved, Wilma found herself getting into the spirit of things. "Try this blend," she suggested to a young couple after telling them Debbie had been deserted on her wedding day. "It's everyone's favorite lemon tea, but we're thinking of calling it 'Her Hopeful Heart.' Seems fitting, don't you think?"

The couple nodded, adding a few packets to their purchase.

Ada and Wilma were astounded by the outpouring of support as the day wore on. It wasn't just about the tea anymore; it was about the community—Amish and *Englishers*—coming together, showing their care and support.

As they were packing up at the day's end, nearly sold out, Ada turned to Wilma. "You know, I think we did something good here today. Not just for Debbie, but for all of us."

Wilma nodded, a smile playing on her lips. "Some-

SAMANTHA PRICE

times, it takes a bit of tea and a lot of sympathy to bring people together."

Ada grabbed Wilma's arm. "Here she comes."

Debbie walked toward them, staring at something in her hand. "I can't believe it," she said when she reached them. "A stall holder I barely know just gave me two hundred dollars for no reason. I tried to give it back, but he insisted I keep it."

Wilma hoped Debbie wouldn't find out what they'd been saying.

Debbie looked up and stared at the stall. "Where's all the tea gone?"

"Most of it has sold," Ada said, dusting off her hands.

"What? All of it?"

"If you don't see it, it's been sold," Wilma said.

Debbie's face brightened. "Wow. You must've had a good day. I'll have to restock the shelves before tomorrow. I'll get more from the storage unit out back."

"No. We'll do that when we come back tomorrow morning."

Wilma nodded. "Yes, and we better make sure we have enough to sell. We're ready for another big day tomorrow."

"All the money wouldn't fit in the cash tin, so we had to put it in shopping bags."

Debbie's mouth fell open when she saw the bags of money. "Oh my. I haven't seen that much in a long time."

"It'll help with your new life."

"It certainly will. Are you sure it's not too much for the both of you to come back tomorrow?" Debbie inquired.

"We'll do this for the next week or two," Ada insisted. "That's what we said we'd do to give you enough time to get settled."

Debbie grinned. "Thank you. I didn't know you two were such good salesladies."

"Nothing to it. People didn't know they needed more tea in their lives," Ada said with a laugh.

"Needed more tea?" Debbie asked.

"Yes. Exactly."

"This is unbelievable. I don't know why this is all happening." Debbie stood there staring at Ada and Wilma. "Is there something going on?"

"Like what?" Ada blinked rapidly.

"I'm sensing something is not quite right. You both look guilty."

"We might as well tell her, Ada. You see, we suggested different names for the tea. The lemon tea, we hinted that it was going to be renamed Her Hopeful Heart."

Ada quickly caught on. "And then another one we renamed the Relaxation Blend. What flavor was that one again, Wilma?"

Debbie's eyebrows rose. "That's interesting. Do you think the suggested name changes helped sell all that tea?"

Wilma nodded enthusiastically. "I can't think what else."

"Hmm. I'll have to talk with the man who helps me with the blending and packaging. He's great at marketing. I'll see what he thinks about changing some names. It'll be costly to change the packaging, but it might be worth it."

"How old is this man?" Ada asked.

Wilma dug Ada in the ribs. "He's not one of us, Ada. Is he, Debbie?"

"No. He's an *Englisher,* and he's quite old. Besides, I'm not looking for anyone right now or possibly ever." A smile hinted around Debbie's lips. "Let's go home. I'll help restock in the morning."

"No. We'll do that. No need for you to be here at all."

"And we'll drive ourselves here and back home again," Wilma added.

"No, we'll have Samuel bring us," Ada said with a nod. "It'll give him something to do."

Ada and Wilma gathered their things and headed toward Debbie's horse and buggy, a sense of accomplishment between them.

Wilma settled into the backseat, and Ada sat in the front. Debbie took the reins, and they started their journey home. The clop-clop of the horse's hooves on the road provided a comforting rhythm to their ride.

Looking back at the market fading into the distance, Ada broke the silence. "You know, I think we made a difference today. Not just in sales, but in lifting your mood, Debbie."

HER HOPEFUL HEART

Debbie smiled. "I can't argue with that. I was dreading facing everyone here in case they'd heard about... you know. But today, it felt like the whole town was behind me. When I walked into the markets, everyone was smiling at me. Wait, you didn't say anything to anyone, did you?"

"Someone asked, I think. Now, what did you do today, Debbie?" Wilma asked, hoping to change the subject.

"I spent most of the day unpacking and figuring out where things should go. I'm so happy for a fresh start."

Ada nodded encouragingly. "A fresh start is good. And we're here to help every step of the way."

The buggy turned onto a quieter street, the houses becoming more spaced out as they approached the outskirts of town.

"Today made me realize something," Debbie continued, her gaze fixed on the road ahead.

"What's that?" Ada asked.

"I'm okay on my own."

"Me too," Wilma said.

As they reached Wilma's house, Debbie said, "I have to ask again. Did anyone mention Fritz or what happened at my wedding that wasn't really a wedding?"

Ada opened her mouth to speak but then glanced over her shoulder at Wilma, who was in the back seat.

"No one mentioned Fritz's name that I can remember," Wilma said.

"Not one person," Ada added.

"That's good. The sooner everyone forgets about it,

the better. I'm still shocked that someone gave me two hundred dollars. I wonder why he did that?"

"Maybe *Gott* knew you needed it, Debbie."

"Possibly."

CHAPTER 21

The very next day, while Wilma and Ada were busy working at the tea stall, dreaming up new stories to tell, Debbie retreated to her cottage.

Debbie's day was dedicated to the seemingly endless task of unpacking.

She was methodically sorting through her belongings when she heard the familiar sound of a horse and buggy. She peeked through the window and saw Gabe.

As Debbie stepped outside, Gabe greeted her with a warm, friendly smile. "I saw the horse and buggy and knew you were here. I thought I'd stop by and see how you're settling in. How's the new horse doing?"

Debbie, leaning against the doorframe, couldn't help but smile at Gabe's thoughtful gesture. "He's great, really settling in well. He's at Wilma's house. Samuel wants to try him first. He's doing that today for me," she replied.

"Great idea."

"I've been meaning to thank you again for helping me choose him. I couldn't have made such a good decision without your help."

"I was happy to help. It allowed me to get to know Eli and Samuel better." Gabe gestured toward the boxes on the porch. "I'm sure you've got a lot to do, and I've got to get back to work."

"Thanks for stopping by, Gabe. It's always good to see a friendly face."

As Gabe climbed back into his buggy, he turned to Debbie. "You know, if you need any help or want some company, don't hesitate to ask."

"Thanks, Gabe." Debbie waved as his horse and buggy moved away. She stepped toward the house but stopped when she saw a taxi turning into her driveway.

She frowned, wondering who it could be. When it got closer, she recognized the familiar figure in the backseat.

Fritz!

CHAPTER 22

*D*ebbie held her breath as Fritz got out of the passenger side of the taxi.

He didn't look happy. He turned and glared at Gabe's retreating horse and buggy before turning to Debbie. "Moved on pretty quickly, I see. New house and a new man, huh?"

Debbie shook her head. "He's just a friend. Nothing more," she said firmly.

There was a tense pause before Fritz spoke again, "Can we talk, Debbie?"

She hesitated, then nodded slowly. "Of course. Um." She glanced at her house, not wanting to invite him into her newfound sanctuary. "We can sit on the porch."

He nodded at the driver, and the driver turned off the engine.

They sat down, the cold air creating a physical barrier as much as the emotional one between them.

Debbie wrapped her arms around herself, partly against the chill, partly in a protective gesture.

Fritz looked at her, his eyes searching. "I... I know I owe you an explanation."

"Yes, you do. You left me looking like a fool, Fritz. Do you have any idea how I feel?"

Fritz sighed, his gaze dropping. "I know it was wrong, and I'm sorry. I panicked, got scared of... of everything changing."

"So you decided not to show up? To leave me there, wondering what I did wrong?"

He shook his head. "It wasn't you. It was me, my fears. It was about everything that was happening in my life. I wasn't ready, but it wasn't about you."

Debbie let out a bitter laugh. "Not ready? We talked about our future. We made plans. We had a house we were going to move to."

"I know, and I regret it every day," Fritz said, his voice low. "I wrote the note because I didn't want to go to Wilma's house to talk with you. It would've made too much of a fuss, and I didn't want people trying to talk me out of my decision."

Debbie looked away. "And why are you here now?"

He hesitated. "I don't want to tell you everything that's going on in my life right now. I can say I'm sorry."

Debbie's gaze met his. "Do you think an apology is enough after what you did?"

"I don't expect anything. I just needed you to know, to hear the truth from me."

There was a long silence as she processed his

words. Finally, she spoke. "I've started a new life here. One that I'm building on my own. I can't go back to what we had. Anyway, what is the truth? Why did you leave?"

He shuffled his feet, looking down. "I made a decision, be it right or wrong. I can see you've moved on, so maybe I made the right decision for both of us."

She frowned, a mix of anger and disbelief in her voice. "Moved on? Why wouldn't I after what you did? You left me a note, Fritz. A note! Jared had been playing pranks with similar notes, so we all thought it was just another one of his games. We waited for you, not knowing you had left town. I came down Wilma's stairs expecting to meet you at the bottom. You were nowhere, and no one knew anything."

Fritz looked away from her. "Things are happening, things I couldn't drag you into."

She shook her head, her voice rising. "You could've talked to me, Fritz! We were about to get married. Whatever it was, we could've faced it together!"

He sighed deeply. "I can tell you this much. I have a lot of debt, Debbie. I'm drowning in it. I couldn't let that become your burden, too."

"Debt? That's why you left? Because you were in financial trouble?"

"Yes," he admitted, his voice strained. "I was and still am ashamed. I thought leaving was sparing you from my mess."

Debbie's expression softened slightly, but the hurt was still there. "But we would've been a team. We could've worked through it. My tea business is increasing every day. We would've found a way through it together."

Fritz shook his head, regret written all over his face. "I can't see any way out that doesn't involve hurting you."

"I wanted to be involved though."

"Wanted, but not now?" he questioned.

She stared at him, wondering if he'd come back for a second chance. He said he'd come to apologize. She held her head in her hands. Part of her wanted him back. The other, more minor, part of her didn't want to forgive him.

CHAPTER 23

Debbie knew she had to express herself to him. She'd been given this chance to speak her mind and she was going to do it. "You were the one who left me. It's not the attitude I want the man I marry to have. The man I marry will consider my feelings. We'll be a team."

He frowned. "A team? Marriage is not volleyball."

Silence enveloped them, heavy with the weight of past decisions and lost opportunities. Debbie finally spoke. "And now? Why come back now?"

Fritz looked up, meeting her gaze. "I've been trying to sort out my life, to deal with my debts. I wanted to explain everything to you. Maybe I was hoping for some softness and forgiveness."

Debbie took a deep breath, the past and present colliding in her heart. "Forgiveness isn't easy, not after everything. You left Jared, too. And I've had to pick up the pieces."

"I understand," he whispered. "I just needed you to know the truth. I never stopped loving you. What I did was rash. I hope you'll give me another chance. We could get married quietly and quickly and forget the past. God says to forgive."

Debbie stood up. "I appreciate your honesty but would've appreciated it when it mattered. I can't, Fritz, I just can't. I can work on forgiving you, but I think it will be a process."

"Hmm." Fritz glared at her. "Does this answer of yours have anything to do with that man that just left?"

"Oh, him? He's a friend. No. Nothing to do with him at all or with anyone. I'm just trying to tell you how I feel. I'm being honest with you like I hoped you'd be honest with me."

"Hmm," he murmured once more.

"And, you have no right to ask me about any man from now on. You had your chance. We could've been happily married by now. I'm sorry, but the door that was once open to you is now closed."

Fritz nodded slowly, a sad acceptance in his eyes. "I'm not happy about that guy swooping in on you." He shook his head. "It's not right. I'm going to talk with the bishop about him." Fritz stood up.

"Yes, good idea. Talk with the bishop about him because he's actually staying with the bishop."

Fritz's mouth fell open.

"I told you nothing is going on. I need no man to replace you. I'm fine on my own."

He moved closer, and Debbie's breath caught in her

throat. Old feelings came rushing back as his fingertips gently touched her cheek.

"You're not the kind of woman who will do well alone. You need a man. You went straight from my brother to me. I don't think you've ever been on your own."

"I am now." Debbie swallowed hard, hoping she wouldn't weaken. He didn't deserve it.

Fritz stared at her, turned, and headed to the waiting taxi.

Debbie remained on the porch, watching the car disappear into the distance.

His visit had stirred up wounds that she'd been trying to heal. She had found herself wanting to be in his arms just now.

When she was about to walk into the house, the taxi returned.

Fritz jumped out and walked back to her.

She took a deep breath and held it.

When he got to a few feet in front of her, he said, "I know I should have talked to you. But at that time, it felt like I was protecting you. It's hard for a man to admit his business is failing."

Debbie felt a surge of frustration. "Protecting me? By leaving me with no explanation? Do you have any idea how humiliating that was?"

"Look. There's no point going over the same thing all the time. Yes, you got hurt and embarrassed, but I'm here now. I came back to you." When she said nothing, he continued, "There are things in my life, complications, that I didn't want you to get caught up in."

Debbie crossed her arms, her voice tinged with bitterness. "So instead, you chose to break my heart? To leave me questioning everything we had?"

He looked up, his eyes filled with regret. "Here is the truth, Debbie. If I married you, it would become your burden, too. I couldn't do that to you."

"Is that why you left? Because you were afraid of burdening me?"

"Yes," Fritz admitted. "Things are getting worse. I employed people, but they didn't do what they were supposed to be doing. One man didn't show up at work at all. He said he was lunching with people and networking and still put his hand out for his pay." Fritz shook his head. "I fired him, and then I was charged with unlawful dismissal."

"How does that work?" Debbie asked.

"The system is flawed. It leans to the side of the employee. Then, I also had another fellow who needed help to follow instructions. He was told to reply briefly to emails, but he did two pages worth of replies to each inquiry, wasting valuable time. He showed me, thinking I'd be pleased. I have had a challenging time employing people, dragging everything down. It is all their fault. They did this to me. I had to take out loans to keep everything afloat."

Debbie looked away, processing his words. She didn't say it, but she was aware he was taking no responsibility and blaming other people. "You should have trusted me. We could have found a way."

"I know that now," he said softly. "I thought early on in our courtship that you could work for me after we married, but you've got your tea business. The best thing I could think of was having a wife who could work with me."

"So I wasn't your ideal wife because I wasn't going to work in your business?"

"Do you want the truth or not?" He stared at her.

"I do, but I'm sad the truth is so horrible. Did you want a wife or an employee?"

"I thought I was sparing you." There was a silence between them, filled with unspoken words and shared memories. "I've been trying to fix things, to get my life back on track. I wanted to see you to explain. I hoped for a reconciliation or some forgiveness."

"You said that already. I don't know if I can give you that. What you did, it changed everything. It changed me."

"I understand," Fritz said, his voice barely a whisper. "I just needed you to know the truth. That it was never about not loving you. But I can see it hasn't affected you that much."

Debbie's mouth fell open. "Not affect me that much? You have no idea what you've done to me."

"Tell me the truth. Who was that fellow here just now? Why is he staying with the bishop? Has he been in trouble with the law? You can't be mixing with criminals."

"If you'd been around, you would've known who he was. But you've been away too much. Now I know why. I wish you the best, Fritz. I hope you find your way out of your troubles. Please go now."

"Is that what you really want?"

Debbie nodded. "More than anything. Goodbye."

As Fritz walked away, Debbie sat back down, the coldness of the day seeping into her bones.

CHAPTER 24

*D*ebbie hadn't been able to bring herself to tell anyone that Fritz had been back to speak with her. The last thing she wanted was to hear one hundred and one opinions about what happened and advice on how she should've handled it.

Since she hadn't heard or seen Fritz in several days, she'd assumed he'd gone home.

She was back at her tea stall working alongside Wilma and Ada, wrapping a package of tea for Mrs. Hensley when she saw Fritz approaching through the crowd. His eyes were fixed on her, a mix of lingering guilt and something unreadable in his gaze.

The chatter around the stall dimmed as he neared. Debbie felt a knot tighten in her stomach. Fritz stopped before her, and she could feel Wilma and Ada move closer behind her. When Mrs. Hensley saw him, she handed over her money, grabbed the package, and hurried away without a word.

"Debbie," he began, his voice hesitant. "I know I'm the last person you want to see, but can we talk?"

Debbie, gripping the edge of the stall's table, steadied herself. "What could you possibly say that you haven't said already?"

Ada stepped forward. "What are you doing back here, Fritz?"

Before Fritz could respond, the unexpected unfolded. Two police officers' badges gleaming, weaved through the market crowd toward them. Their expressions were stern, their purpose clear.

Fritz's eyes widened in alarm as they approached. "Fritz White," one officer announced firmly, "you are under arrest for tax fraud and evasion."

A ripple of shock passed through the onlookers. Ada grabbed Wilma's arm and clung to it as Fritz sputtered in disbelief, "There's been a mistake. This can't be happening."

The officer continued, unaffected by Fritz's protests. "You need to come with us."

As they handcuffed him, murmurs and whispers swirled through the bystanders. Debbie watched, her heart pounding.

Fritz, now in handcuffs, turned to Debbie. "I never meant for any of this. Believe me."

The officers led him away before he could say more, leaving a trail of murmurs in their wake. The market slowly resumed its rhythm, but the air around Debbie's stall felt heavier, tinged with the drama that had just unfolded.

Wilma rushed to Debbie. "Are you okay?"

Debbie nodded, her eyes following Fritz until he and the officers were out of sight. "I'm fine. It's just... a lot to take in. He did tell me the other day he had financial concerns."

"You saw him the other day?" Ada asked.

"He came a few days ago and tried to explain himself. I didn't tell anyone because I didn't want to dredge it all up again. I just wanted to forget everything."

Wilma patted her arm. "We understand."

"We do," Ada agreed. "I've never seen a man arrested before. So that's how it's done."

Wilma frowned at Ada.

"I mean. You had an escape then, Debbie," Ada said.

"I know. It was all for the best," Debbie said. "I'm realizing that now."

The rest of the day passed in a blur for Debbie. Customers came with words of comfort, some with stories of their own heartaches—no one left without purchasing Debbie's tea.

CHAPTER 25

As news of Fritz's arrest spread like wildfire through the community, it wasn't long before it reached Florence and Carter.

Later that evening, Carter arrived at Wilma's house, where Debbie, Ada, and a few others had gathered.

With a solemn expression, Carter began, "I did some digging on Fritz's case. It's as serious as it gets. He's facing a hefty fine, up to $100,000. The fine could escalate to half a million if his business was incorporated. And that's not all—he could be looking at up to five years in jail."

The room fell silent as the gravity of the situation sank in. Debbie, who had been quietly listening, felt a complex mix of emotions. The man she had once loved was now entangled in a legal battle that could change his life drastically. 'I can't believe it's happening."

"Maybe he knew this was coming, and that's why he left," Krystal suggested.

"Let's not make any excuses for why he did what he did to Debbie," Ada said.

Wilma added, "This is unfortunate, but perhaps it's for the best. Debbie, you're free from this now. It's a fresh start."

Ada nodded. "That's right. We're not happy he did this to you, but you must make the best of a bad situation. You've got a new path ahead of you, and we're all here to support you."

Debbie looked over at Carter. "Do you think he'll go to jail?"

He shrugged his shoulders. "I'm not sure. It depends on a lot of different factors."

For the first time, Debbie was pleased that he'd walked out on her. "Could marrying me have helped him with his tax somehow?"

"It could've. He could've spread some income by putting it in your name."

Debbie bit her lip. "I wonder if that's why he wanted to marry me in the first place. Maybe he never loved me at all. Then the guilt set in, and he decided…"

Ada squeezed Debbie's hand reassuringly. "Whether he loved you or not, what he did was wrong. You deserve someone who wants you for you, not for financial gain."

Carter nodded in agreement. "It's good you're not entangled in his legal troubles now. You could've been dragged into it if you had married him."

The room was filled with mixed emotions: anger, sympathy, and a sense of justice. Debbie's heart-breaking situation had thankfully kept her away from the legal quagmire that Fritz was sinking into.

Krystal, who had been quiet, said, "Debbie, you're strong. You've handled all of this with such calmness. I would've been throwing things and shouting."

"Well, I've felt like it at times." A smile crept onto Debbie's lips.

"Just as well, you're a calm person."

Ada leaned over and whispered to Wilma, "Maybe the calm before the storm."

∽

THE FOLLOWING MORNING, Debbie took the last of her and Jared's things to her new house. After she had unpacked half a dozen boxes, she moved out to the porch for a rest. It was chilly out there, but she loved watching the world go by. This house was hers, giving her a certain sense of satisfaction.

When she heard a horse and buggy, Debbie looked over and was surprised when it turned into her driveway and even more surprised to see Gabe.

A smile touched her lips. "Morning, Gabe," she greeted, her voice carrying a hint of weariness. "I guess you think I do nothing all day but sit out here."

He laughed. "Well, I was wondering…"

"I'm having a break from unpacking the last of my things. I'm officially moving in today."

"That's great. I'm happy for you." He beamed a smile at her.

"Thank you."

"I heard about Fritz," he began. "I'm sorry, Debbie. That must have been hard to see."

"You mean the arrest?"

"Yes."

Debbie sighed. "It was a shock, for sure. I just never expected things to end like this."

Gabe nodded. "Sometimes life throws us things we never see coming. How are you holding up?"

Considering his question, Debbie looked out at the gentle sway of the trees in her yard. "I'm getting there, day by day. It helps to know I have support from friends, family... and the community."

"And what about Jared?"

"He doesn't show much emotion. He'll love living here. He loves his room, and he's closer to school, so it's not as far for him to walk. He definitely likes that." Debbie glanced around her porch, her eyes landing on a few potted herbs that needed to be planted. An idea sparked in her mind. "Gabe, I could use a hand with something if you don't mind staying longer. I've been meaning to find a spot to plant those. I could use your advice."

Gabe looked at the herbs — basil, thyme, mint — and then at Debbie with a friendly smile. "I'd be happy to help out. I might not be a gardening expert, but I have a few ideas. That spot by the side of your house looks like it might have been a vegetable garden once. We could freshen up the soil, which would be perfect for your herbs."

As Debbie's eyes followed Gabe's pointing finger, she noticed the small patch of earth he was referring to. It did look promising, a forgotten piece of land that could be revitalized. "I'd also like to plant some flowers there, add a little color," she mused aloud.

"I've got time now if you want to make a start."

"I'd love that. It sounds more rewarding than unpacking. Anyway, I'm nearly done with that."

"Got a shovel?"

"Yes. I saw a few tools in the back of the buggy. I'll have to return them to Eli, but I'm sure he won't mind if I borrow them."

"Let's get started then." He walked to the buggy and grabbed the shovel and a rake. "The first step is to loosen up this soil. It's been untended for a while."

The two of them began to work on the garden, with Gabe showing Debbie how to aerate the soil properly. As they worked, Debbie carefully considered where each plant should go. "The basil needs a lot of sun. Maybe it should go in this spot," she suggested, pointing to an area further away from the house.

"That sounds like a good plan," Gabe replied, digging a small hole for the basil. "And the mint spreads quite a bit, so maybe planting it towards the edge would be best?"

Debbie agreed and handed him the mint. As they continued to plant, their conversation flowed naturally. They chatted about everything from the best way to water plants to their favorite types of flowers. It was a simple yet engaging task that allowed them to relax and enjoy the moment.

Every so often, Debbie stepped back to admire their handiwork. "You said you weren't an expert. You've done pretty well. You are currently working in an orchard, so you must've learned a bit."

Gabe chuckled. "I guess so. I'm enjoying it."

As they planted the last of the herbs, Debbie couldn't help but feel grateful for Gabe's assistance. "It's been nice having you here to help."

Gabe looked around at their progress. "It's looking great, Debbie. These plants are going to thrive here."

"I think so."

They both stood momentarily, looking at the small garden they had brought to life.

"I should go back to work. Just give me a shout if you need more help with this garden or anything else."

Debbie nodded, appreciating his offer. "Thanks, Gabe. I haven't even offered you a coffee or anything. I feel dreadful. I'm a bad hostess."

Gabe flashed a friendly smile. "No, you're not. I don't need anything. We've got a good community here; we look out for each other." He gave a casual wave as he started walking back to his buggy. "See you around!"

Debbie watched him leave, thinking about his words. Gabe had said, 'We've got a good community here.' Did that mean he was planning on staying?

CHAPTER 26

When Gabe left, Debbie unpacked the rest of Jared's clothes. Then she heard a knock on the door. She thought it was Gabe again, but when she opened the door, she saw the bishop.

"Debbie," he greeted her. "How have you been?"

"Good morning, Bishop Paul. I'm... getting there. The move into the cottage has been a big change, but it was the right decision. It's a bit scary, navigating everything on my own, but I know it's for the best."

The bishop nodded understandingly, taking a seat on the porch. She sat beside him. "Change, even when it's for the better, can be daunting. I hope you've gotten over what happened."

A lump formed in Debbie's throat. Being dumped on her wedding day was something she knew would never leave her. It was another scar on her heart, much like her secret marriage to Jared's father. All she could do was nod.

After a moment of silence, the bishop continued, "I have some news about Fritz. I went to see if there was any way I could help with bail or to offer some support."

Debbie hadn't been sure if the bishop had heard about Fritz, but he was the bishop, and eventually, all gossip reached his ears. "How did he seem?"

The bishop sighed. "He refused to speak with me. It seems he's not ready to face anyone from the community, not even for assistance."

Debbie absorbed the information. "I suppose I'm not surprised," she finally said. "After everything that's happened, maybe he's too ashamed. Or maybe he doesn't want help because it will drag other people in."

The bishop nodded. "It's a difficult situation, and everyone handles these things in their own way. The most important thing is that you focus on your path forward."

"I'm doing that. This house is a new chapter for me and Jared, and I'm ready to make the most of it."

"You're not working today?"

"No. Wilma and Ada have worked at the tea stall for me for a while. They insisted."

"That's a good idea. Have a rest and clear your head. Debbie, what Fritz did to you... I've never seen it happen before. I know it must be hard."

Debbie hung her head. "I just want everyone to forget it. I fear that everyone will be talking about it for years to come. They'll say, 'Remember that time when

Fritz White changed his mind about marrying Debbie Bruner.'" She cringed at the thought.

"We can't worry about that, but you can stop worrying about what people say and think."

The bishop's wisdom and calm words made her feel a lot better. "Thanks. I need to remember that."

"I'll leave you with that thought. If you need anything, you know where I am. Hannah wanted to come, but she's had the flu." The bishop stood up.

"Oh, I hope she feels better soon."

The bishop smiled, gave her a nod, and headed back to his horse and buggy.

As soon as the bishop left, the gentle pitter-patter of rain began to sprinkle down.

She walked inside, her thoughts turning inward. Everything was very still without the daily bustle of the farmers market. She wandered into the living room, where unpacked boxes still sat in corners, their contents waiting to find their new places.

Debbie tidied up, picked up a few stray items, and folded a blanket left on the couch. As she moved about, her mind wandered back to the lively atmosphere of the market—the chatter of customers, the friendly banter with other vendors, and the sense of purpose each sale brought.

The quiet of the house seemed to amplify her thoughts. At the market, there was always someone to talk to, always something to do. Here, in the stillness of her own space, she confronted a sudden loneliness she hadn't anticipated.

Debbie moved to the kitchen, thinking she should have gone to work today. She washed up a few dishes that were left over from breakfast.

She dried her hands on a towel and leaned against the counter, looking around the kitchen. This was her space now, and she could organize it just as she wanted. There was no going along with, 'This should be placed here' or 'This is always there.' Everything was up to her for the first time in her adult life. It was a strange yet liberating feeling.

CHAPTER 27

Cherish and Malachi sat side by side at their kitchen table, a single pregnancy test lying before them. The air was thick with anticipation, each second stretching out longer than the last. As they waited for the result, their hands found each other's.

She was hoping that this time, it would be positive. It would be hard to cope with another disappointment. She didn't want her child to be too much younger than Favor's.

Finally, Malachi reached for the pregnancy test stick. His hand was steady, but Cherish could feel the slight tremor of his excitement. He turned it over, and there it was, a positive result.

Cherish blinked a couple of times and stared hard to ensure she wasn't seeing things.

A wave of emotion washed over both of them.

"It's positive," Malachi whispered. "We're going to have a baby. We'll be parents."

Cherish's eyes brimmed with tears, a smile spreading across her face. "I can hardly believe it. We're going to be parents!"

A single tear escaped, tracing a path down Malachi's cheek. "I have so many dreams for our child," he said, his voice quivering slightly. "I want to teach them about the land, about our way of life. I want them to feel the same love and peace I've found with you."

Cherish laughed. "Them? We're starting with one."

"We'll have loads of children."

Cherish leaned into him, her head resting on his shoulder. "And I can't wait to see you as a father and our little one grow. This child will be a part of us, a blend of our love and faith."

They sat together in comfortable silence, each lost in thoughts of the future – of late-night lullabies, of tiny hands holding theirs, of lives forever changed.

Cherish started worrying. "Oh, I hope that the test isn't faulty."

Malachi's eyes widened. "Do you think it could be?"

Cherish bit her lip. "I bought a bunch ages ago, so I had plenty. It's embarrassing to buy them. So I bought a lot at the one time. What if they've expired?"

"If you've got more, try another one. And check the expiration date."

Cherish raced out of the room. She came back a few minutes later. They waited again.

"Positive!" Malachi yelled out, waking Wally and Caramel in the process.

Cherish covered her mouth and giggled. "I can barely believe it after all this time."

As the moment settled, Cherish's thoughts turned to her sister, Favor. "I need to tell Favor. She's going to be so thrilled."

Malachi nodded. "I'll hitch the buggy for you," he offered, standing up. "She should be the first to know, after us. Then your mother will be the next."

"Of course." Cherish watched as Malachi moved with purpose as he headed out the door. She quickly freshened up, and soon joined him outside.

Cherish insisted on going alone to deliver the news. The ride to Favor's house was a blur, the landscape passing in awhirl. She thought she should take a third test before telling anyone, but then she reflected on other signs she'd had. Surely two tests couldn't be wrong.

Upon arriving, Cherish rushed to Favor's door and knocked eagerly.

CHAPTER 28

Harriet met Cherish at the door and led her into the living room. She gestured towards the couch with a warm smile. "You two have a nice talk while I get us something to drink. How about some hot chocolate?"

"That sounds perfect, Harriet, thanks," Cherish replied, settling into the plush cushions.

"I thought you weren't coming here today," Favor said.

"Well, I'm here, and I have some news."

Favor looked at her with a mix of curiosity and amusement. "Good news or bad news? You don't look sad, so I guess no one has died unless you don't like someone."

Cherish playfully hit Favor's arm. "Good news, of course! Why would you even ask?"

Favor chuckled. "Alright, spill it. What's going on?"

Leaning in closer, Cherish could hardly contain her

excitement. "I'm pregnant!" she exclaimed. "I took a test, and it was positive. Then I took another, and it was too."

Favor's eyes widened in surprise and delight. "Oh, Cherish! That's amazing. I'm so happy for you!"

Cherish's face beamed. "I can't believe it myself. I was starting to think it would never happen for us and that I'd have to be one of those aunts that doted on their nieces and nephews."

Favor took Cherish's hands in hers. "Our kids are going to grow up together! Can you imagine? Just like we did."

Cherish nodded. "Exactly! They'll be best friends, just like us. It's like a dream come true."

"Have you told anyone yet?" Favor asked.

"Only you so far."

"Then I need to ask you something. I want this to be our little secret for now. At least, until after my baby is born."

Cherish's smile faltered. "But why? This is such wonderful news. I'm bursting to tell everyone."

Favor huffed. "I've always been overlooked, being the fifth daughter. You, being the youngest, got all the attention. You were the baby, the one everyone fussed over. I'm enjoying getting the attention now that I'm pregnant, and if people find out about you, I'll be overlooked again."

Cherish listened, her heart sinking as she tried to understand Favor's point of view. "I see."

"This is the first time in my life that I've felt like I

truly matter, like people are genuinely interested in me and my life," Favor continued.

Cherish reached for Favor's hand, her own heart aching with empathy. "I never knew you felt that way," she murmured.

Favor nodded. "Having this baby, it's my moment, Cherish. It's the first time I've felt the family's focus solely on me. I don't want to share the attention just yet, not until my baby is here. And you don't want to tell people too soon, do you?"

"Don't I?"

Favor shook her head. "No. You normally wait three months before you tell anyone just to be safe."

"Safe?" Cherish asked.

"Yes, safe."

"Oh. And by that time, your baby will be born."

"Exactly."

Cherish nodded. "Okay. I won't say a word until after your baby is born."

As Cherish and Favor sat entwined in their intimate conversation, the sudden entrance of Harriet, Favor's mother-in-law, broke the peaceful atmosphere of the living room, carrying a tray of three hot chocolates and a plate of cookies.

"Cherish, did I hear something about you being pregnant?" Harriet's inquisitive gaze settled on Cherish.

Cherish's eyebrows shot up in surprise. In a split second, she weighed her options. Revealing her secret was out of the question, seeing she had promised

SAMANTHA PRICE

Favor. Thinking quickly, she deflected the conversation. "I can't remember saying that word, but look at Favor here. She's the one who's pregnant!" Cherish gently placed her hand on Favor's belly, drawing Harriet's attention to her daughter-in-law. "And no one can miss that now. Look how big she is. You must be getting excited, Harriet. You'll be a grandmother in no time."

Harriet's face lit up with joy, her earlier suspicion melting away. "Oh, indeed. We're all buzzing with excitement. We can barely wait for the new arrival."

"I certainly can't wait," Cherish said.

Harriet chatted about the little garments she had started knitting and the nursery that they were setting up. Eventually, Harriet paused, her eyes twinkling with an idea. "You know what? This calls for a celebration. I'll get us some chocolate cake. I remember, Cherish, how much you love chocolate."

"I do."

Cherish and Favor exchanged a quick, relieved glance as Harriet bustled back to the kitchen.

"That was a good save," Favor whispered.

"Thanks, but what are we celebrating? She must think I'm pregnant. She'll tell Ada and *Mamm* for sure."

"She won't. Besides, you never said you were, so she'd look a fool if she told anyone something she doesn't know for certain."

"I guess. I hope so anyway."

"Thanks for agreeing to keep it a secret for now, Cherish. Does Malachi know?"

Cherish burst out laughing. Then, she remembered to keep her voice down. "Of course he does."

"What did he say? I would've loved to have seen his face."

"He was excited. He didn't say much. I was sure I saw a tear in his eye."

Favor covered her mouth to stifle a giggle. "No."

"Yes."

As Harriet returned with a tray laden with slices of rich chocolate cake, the atmosphere in the room shifted to one of celebration and comfort. The three women sat together, their conversation ebbing and flowing around family, motherhood, and the changes a new baby would bring.

Cherish listened, taking everything in and participating in the conversation while grappling internally with her own news. She felt a tinge of guilt for not sharing her pregnancy, but a stronger sense of loyalty to Favor held her back. She knew her time would come, but it was Favor's moment for now.

CHAPTER 29

Cherish had just gotten back home when she heard the phone in the barn ringing. She answered and listened to the unmistakable excitement in her mother's voice. "Cherish, Mercy is pregnant. She's having baby number three. I've just learned about it now. We're all so thrilled! She's the first of you girls to have a third child."

Cherish was genuinely happy for Mercy, yet she couldn't help feeling disappointed at being unable to share her news. Also, Favor would be most upset about sharing her moment. "That's so exciting. I'm happy for her."

"You don't sound pleased," Wilma said.

"I am. It's great news. When's the baby due?" Cherish asked.

"I don't know for certain yet. She said it's early days."

Cherish would've loved to tell her mother that there

was yet another grandchild on the way, but she had to keep her word.

"I must go. I've got other people to call. Bye now."

Cherish heard the phone click in her ear. Then she replaced the receiver and saw that Malachi had just entered the barn. "I need to go see Favor again. I've just heard something she should know."

"I'll come back with you. I promised to help Simon and Melvin with something." Together, they set off toward Favor's place.

"So, what's this thing you have to tell her?" Malachi asked.

"Mercy's having another baby."

"That's great news!"

"No, it's not." Cherish shook her head while all kinds of emotions rushed through her.

"It's not?" Malachi asked.

"No. Well, it is, but it isn't."

"Why?"

"Because I'm supposed to keep quiet about our baby because Favor wants all of *Mamm's* attention. Now Favor will be upset, and I'm upset too." Cherish folded her arms.

Malachi glanced over at her. "You're not making any sense."

Cherish felt tears stinging behind her eyes. "It's simple. Favor never got any attention as a child. Now she's getting a lot from *Mamm,* and *Mamm* was going to visit. But now, will she visit, or will she go and see Mercy? And, all the while, I've got to be quiet about our baby. And why should I? Because it's our first, and I am excited?"

"Don't people normally wait awhile before telling anyone?"

"Yes. You're right. That's what Favor suggested, too." Cherish's bottom lip quivered.

"Then what's the problem?"

"Nothing. Everything."

"Hmm. That's as clear as mud."

Cherish looked out the window at the fields they were passing. As much as she loved Malachi, he didn't understand her sometimes.

Arriving at Favor's, they found the men busy outside with the alpacas, absorbed in their work. While Malachi joined the men, Cherish headed to the house.

After Harriet let her in, she attended to household tasks. Favor was in her usual position on the couch. This time, she was knitting rather than doing nothing.

Cherish waited for the right moment, biding her time until Harriet stepped out of the room. Turning to Favor, she chose her words carefully. "Have you heard about Mercy?"

Favor's face contorted with concern. "What's happened?"

"She's pregnant. *Mamm* just called and told me," Cherish revealed gently.

A look of dismay washed over Favor's face. "Oh no. She promised she wouldn't tell yet."

Cherish was taken aback. "You knew Mercy was pregnant and didn't tell me?"

Favor kept her voice low. "I was there when she found out. I promised to keep it a secret. She didn't want to overshadow Debbie's wedding, and then... I asked her to wait longer so she wouldn't overshadow me. Now she has."

"I'm so sorry, Favor. I had yet to learn about any of this. She is selfish."

Favor, sighing deeply, tried to mask her disappointment with a strained smile. "It's okay, Cherish. It's happy news, after all. It surprised me that she'd go against what she told me. I won't let it upset me, and you shouldn't either."

"It's just disappointing."

CHAPTER 30

Outside, the men's voices and laughter drifted in a reminder of the life that continued around them, oblivious to the complexities of the pregnancy announcements.

"So, do you still want me to wait until you have the baby before I tell anyone?" Cherish asked.

"Of course. Don't worry, it won't be long. Is that okay?"

Their conversation was abruptly interrupted by the men's voices as Malachi, Simon, and Melvin stepped inside, their faces flushed from the work with the alpacas. "We could use some of that famous hot chocolate, Harriet," Malachi called out, his voice breaking the tension in the room.

Harriet, emerging from the kitchen with a tray laden with steaming mugs and slices of cake, smiled warmly at the men. "I thought you might need this," she said, placing the tray on the table. "I'm way ahead of you."

As everyone gathered around, savoring the refreshments, the room filled with light-hearted chatter, a welcome distraction from the earlier conversation. Cherish tried to join in, but her thoughts drifted back to her predicament.

In a quiet moment, Harriet leaned in toward Cherish and Favor, her voice low. "I overheard your conversation earlier," she confessed, her eyes kind yet knowing. "About Mercy's news and your own, Cherish."

Cherish's heart skipped a beat, her eyes meeting Harriet's. She hadn't expected this twist of events.

Harriet continued, her tone gentle but firm. "I understand both of your concerns. Favor, you deserve to have your moment and Cherish, your news is just as important. But remember, in our family, every new life is a blessing and a cause for celebration, not competition."

Favor and Cherish exchanged glances, the truth in Harriet's words resonating deeply.

Seeing the understanding dawning on their faces, Harriet added, "Why don't we celebrate all the good news together? Let's not keep these wonderful blessings under wraps. The more joy we share, the more it multiplies."

The room fell silent as the men looked over at the women. "What's going on?" Simon asked.

Cherish answered first. "Mercy is having another baby."

"Ah, that's wonderful news," Melvin said.

"Your mother will be pleased about that," Simon said, looking at Favor.

"She's delighted."

"You should call her."

Favor nodded. "I will. I'll go to Cherish's place tomorrow and call *Mamm* and Mercy."

Cherish nodded, feeling awful that she hadn't even thought to call Mercy.

"We need to get a phone, too," Simon told his father.

Melvin nodded. "It's on the list."

When the men finished their refreshments and went outside again, Cherish helped Harriet clean up. "Thanks for not saying anything."

"It's your secret, not mine."

"Thanks, but can you not say anything to *Mamm* or Ada?"

"If they don't ask, I won't tell."

Cherish smiled. Harriet wasn't so bad after all. "I'll tell everyone after Favor has the baby. Maybe a few days after."

Harriet nodded. "Whatever you want."

CHAPTER 31

Debbie had just set the table for her and her young son Jared's first supper in their new cottage. The aroma of meatballs and pasta filled the small dining room. It was a quiet, peaceful evening, or so she thought until a knock at the door broke the tranquility.

Jared's face lit up with excitement. "I'll get it!" he exclaimed, rushing toward the door.

Debbie followed, curious to see who their unexpected visitor might be. As the door swung open, she saw Matthew standing there, holding a bouquet.

Jared immediately asked, "What are the flowers for?"

Matthew looked up at Debbie, a broad grin spreading across his face. "They're for your mother."

Debbie hadn't expected this. The flowers were beautiful, no doubt, but their meaning was unmistakable. Matthew was interested in her, not just as a friend, but as something more. She wasn't sure how to respond without hurting his feelings.

"Thank you, Matthew. That's very kind of you." Debbie forced a smile as she took the flowers from him. "Would you like to join us for dinner?"

Matthew's eyes brightened at the invitation. "I'd love to, thank you."

Debbie had always liked Matthew but had always seen him as a tragic figure regarding love. But her own story was tragic, too, and perhaps even more so.

As they settled around the small dining table, Debbie served the meal, trying to focus on the mundane tasks of pouring drinks and passing dishes.

Throughout the meal, Debbie was more reserved than usual, her mind preoccupied with the implications of Matthew's visit. Jared was oblivious to these adult issues and chattered away happily, keeping the conversation alive.

Matthew complimented Debbie on the meal and tried to prolong eye contact, but she kept looking away.

At some point, she knew she'd have to tell him they could only ever be friends, but not in front of Jared.

As the meal progressed, Jared excitedly shared his latest project. "Matthew, guess what? I'm making birdhouses to give away. Everyone should have a birdhouse, right?"

"That sounds like a wonderful project, Jared. I'm sure everyone will love them."

Encouraged by Matthew's interest, Jared continued,

"Eli helped me with the one I made for *Mamm*. He's really good at making things, and he's gonna help."

"Sounds good. I could help, too. I'm fairly handy when it comes to hammer and nails."

"*Mamm's* been helping people at this charity place with Gabe."

Debbie tensed slightly at the mention of Gabe's name, her fork pausing mid-air. She noticed Matthew's reaction, a slight shift in his expression, almost invisible but there.

Jared continued, "And Gabe knows a lot about horses. He helped *Mamm* choose one to buy."

Debbie felt a flush of awkwardness wash over her. Jared's innocent remarks had revealed more about her life and her interactions with Gabe than she would have liked. She glanced at Matthew, trying to gauge his reaction. His smile was still in place, but his eyes had a new, thoughtful look.

Matthew turned the conversation back to Jared's birdhouses, skilfully steering away from the topic of Gabe. Debbie was grateful for the change in the subject.

After dinner, as they cleared the table, Matthew's offer to help was a relief and a reminder of the evening's complexities. Debbie found herself in a peculiar dance of politeness and reservation, accepting his help but maintaining a careful emotional distance.

When it was time for Matthew to leave, he thanked Debbie for the meal and turned to Jared. "Thanks for telling me about your birdhouses, Jared. I can't wait to see them."

Jared's mention of Gabe had also stirred something in her—a realization of how intertwined Gabe had become in their lives.

"Thank you for the lovely meal, Debbie," he said, his gaze lingering a moment longer on her.

"Thank you for the flowers," Debbie said as she opened the door for him.

"Bye, Matthew," Jared called out.

"I'll see you soon." With that, Matthew walked out the door.

Once he left, Jared brushed his teeth, and Debbie tucked him into bed.

"Oh no," he said.

"What is it?"

"I forgot to show Matthew my room. He would like it. No matter, he can see it next time."

"Yes. Next time." Debbie leaned over and kissed Jared on his forehead. He closed his eyes, and she pulled the quilt up to his chin. "Sweet dreams."

"And you too, *Mamm*."

Debbie moved out of his room, closed the door, and settled onto the couch.

She wasn't sure what the future held or what path she wanted to take, but she knew that any decision would be made carefully, not just for her heart but for the little boy who meant the world to her.

The realization that two men might be vying for her attention was flattering and overwhelming, especially after what had happened with Fritz. It was so good to feel wanted.

Her thoughts drifted to Gabe—his easy smile, helpfulness, and how naturally he fit into the fabric of her daily life. Then back to Matthew, with his thoughtful gestures and the gentle way he had with Jared. Both men brought something different, something appealing.

But Debbie knew she couldn't lead anyone on, not Matthew, Gabe, or herself. She needed to take a step back to understand her own feelings before she could even think about starting a new relationship. She stayed up late that night because Wilma and Ada insisted on working for her at the markets the next day.

CHAPTER 32

Wilma and Ada had made it a tradition to share morning tea twice weekly at Wilma's house with their friends Daphne and Susan. Since they were filling in for Debbie at the markets, they asked Daphne and Susan to meet them there.

Soon after Daphne and Susan had joined Wilma and Ada, they were quickly swept up in the tea-selling rhythm. The stall, always a popular spot, seemed even busier than usual. They noticed, however, that many customers already knew about Debbie's unfortunate experience.

What surprised Daphne and Susan even more was how Wilma and Ada were using Debbie's story as part of their sales pitch. "You know, this is the same tea that helped our dear Debbie get through her tough times," Ada said to one customer with a hint of dramatic flair.

Wilma nodded in agreement, adding, "Yes, a warm

cup of our tea can comfort the soul in times of distress."

Between customers, Daphne and Susan exchanged uneasy glances. Once they had a moment between customers, they couldn't help but question Ada and Wilma's approach. "Do you think Debbie knows you're using her story to sell more tea?" Susan asked, her tone laced with concern.

Ada responded, "I see nothing wrong with it. We're only telling the truth. It's not like we're making up stories. And besides, it's good for business, and the more money, the more Debbie will have for her future. And seeing she might be alone for a long time, she'll need it with young Jared."

Wilma nodded in agreement. "Debbie's story is touching people's hearts. They sympathize, and it makes them feel connected to our tea."

Daphne frowned. "Your tea?"

Wilma put her hand over her mouth and laughed. "Debbie's tea."

Daphne, however, was not convinced. "But doesn't it seem a bit... exploitative? Using someone's personal tragedy for profit?"

Ada shook her head. "We're helping spread the word about what happened to Debbie. It's creating a bond between her and her customers. And Debbie's not here to do it herself."

The conversation was interrupted by another wave of customers, curious about the tea and the story behind it. As Wilma and Ada engaged with them, Daphne and Susan stepped back.

"What do you think?" Susan whispered to Daphne.

"Hmm. On one hand, I understand what they're doing. On the other hand, the moral implications of using a personal and painful experience for gain is rather odd."

"It feels wrong to me."

As the day progressed, the stall saw a steady stream of customers, many of whom expressed their sympathies for Debbie and admiration for the strength of the community's support. Daphne and Susan couldn't help but notice the genuine concern in people's voices and the way they cherished the tea even more, knowing how much of herself Debbie had put into the tea blends.

By the end of the day, as they helped Ada and Wilma pack up the stall, Daphne and Susan were still unsure about the situation. They recognized the complexity of the issue—the intersection of community support, empathy, and the nuances of running a business. It was a delicate balance, one that required careful consideration and sensitivity.

CHAPTER 33

*A*s they walked away from the bustling market, the four women chatted about the day's success, but Daphne and Susan remained thoughtful.

When they said goodbye, Susan got into Daphne's buggy to be taken home. "Do you think we should tell Debbie what's going on?" Susan asked.

Daphne thought about it for a moment. "What if she knows?"

"Do you think she does?"

"I don't know. No, I don't think she'd be comfortable with her story being shared in such a public manner." Daphne drummed her fingertips on her chin. "It's hard to know what to do."

"Let's think about it while we drive."

Daphne took up the buggy lines and moved her horse around to face the road. "Straight to your house, then?"

Susan nodded. "Yes, please."

Daphne clicked the horse forward and moved onto the road.

Susan, her brow furrowed in thought, glanced at Daphne. "I feel like we're in a tough spot. On one hand, Wilma and Ada are doing a great job keeping the business running and helping Debbie financially. But on the other hand, it feels like they're overstepping a boundary."

Daphne nodded, her gaze fixed on the passing scenery. "I agree. It's tricky. Debbie's been through so much already. This could add to her stress if she's not okay with it. And do we want to be responsible for that?"

As they neared Susan's house, Susan spoke up again. "I think we should talk with Debbie. It's better she hears it from us rather than from someone else. She deserves to know, and she should have a say in this."

"You're right," Daphne replied, her decision firm. "Let's plan to visit her tomorrow. We'll gently bring it up and gauge her reaction. We need to be there for her, just like Wilma and Ada are, but in a way that respects her privacy and dignity."

Susan adjusted her glasses. "But we should tell Ada and Wilma that we're going to do that, don't you think?"

"You're right, or we'll be accused of going behind their backs."

Then Susan let out a long, drawn-out sigh. "But you heard them. They see nothing wrong."

"Shall we just do nothing? I mean, the damage has been done."

Susan nodded. "We should probably just keep quiet. It's already too late; you're right. We'll wait and see what happens." Wanting to shift away from the heavier topic, Susan glanced at Daphne with a twinkle in her eye. "Daphne, all this talk about Debbie got me thinking. Who in our community would be a good match for her?"

Daphne, welcoming the lighter subject, smiled. "That's an interesting thought. Debbie's a wonderful person. She deserves someone just as kind and understanding."

"What about Jacob Miller? He's been a widower for a couple of years now, and he's got that gentle way about him. He's also great with kids, which would be perfect for Jared."

Daphne considered the idea. "Jacob is a good man, but I wonder if he's ready to move on. It's not easy after losing someone you love. Though, I could see them together."

The conversation continued as they mused over various eligible bachelors in their community. "There's also Ethan Byler," Susan suggested. "He's around Debbie's age, and he's always been so steady and reliable from what I've seen."

Daphne laughed softly. "Yes, but you know Ethan. He's so shy. He'd need a little push even to start a conversation with Debbie."

The mood had lightened considerably as the buggy

turned onto the road leading to Susan's house. They chatted and laughed, discussing the qualities that would make a good partner for Debbie and how nice it would be to see her find happiness again.

Finally, they pulled up to Susan's house, and Daphne brought the horse to a gentle stop. "Well, it's all just speculation at this point," Susan said as she stepped down from the buggy.

"There's always that new man, Gabe. I haven't talked with him much, but he seems nice."

"Whoever it is, the most important thing is that Debbie and Jared are happy and well-cared for."

Daphne smiled. "Absolutely."

"I'll see you soon. Thanks for the ride. Bye now."

"Bye." Susan stood there waving as Daphne's horse and buggy moved away.

CHAPTER 34

After a long day at the market, Wilma and Ada returned to Wilma's cozy home, feeling satisfied from their successful sales. Still, there was a lingering unease from their earlier conversation with Daphne and Susan. As Wilma busied herself feeding Red, her faithful dog, in the kitchen, Ada leaned against the counter, her expression thoughtful.

"You know, Wilma, I felt like Daphne and Susan were putting a damper on our day. They seemed concerned about us sharing Debbie's story at the stall."

Wilma nodded, her hands deftly measuring out Red's dinner. "I noticed that too. It's like they didn't understand what we were trying to do. We're just trying to help Debbie in our own way."

Ada sighed, watching Red wag his tail in anticipation of his meal. "Exactly. They just didn't get it, Wilma. I think it might be best if we tell them that we'll resume our morning teas with them after we finish our two weeks at the stall."

Wilma placed Red's bowl down, and he immediately devoured all the food. She straightened up, wiping her hands on her apron. "I agree. It seems they disapprove of our approach, but we can't control that. We're doing this for Debbie, and we believe it's the right thing. We don't need their help. We can handle all the customers on our own."

Ada nodded in agreement, her mind already on the days ahead. "It's a pity they don't see it like we do."

Wilma joined Ada at the counter. "As always, you have a solution to our problem. We can catch up with Daphne and Susan later once things settle down."

"And not at the markets," Ada said with a nod.

"Agreed." Wilma and Ada exchanged a smile.

∽

AFTER THEIR HEARTFELT conversation in the kitchen, the evening quiet was interrupted by the unmistakable sound of a horse and buggy pulling up. Wilma and Ada moved to the window, peering out to see who their visitor was.

"It's only Krystal, and she has Jed with her," Wilma observed, a knowing smile crossing her face.

"As always. Those two are never apart these days." Ada leaned in, watching as Jed helped Krystal down from the buggy. "Looks like Jed is staying for dinner again."

HER HOPEFUL HEART

Wilma nodded, watching the young couple approach the house. "I wonder when they'll tell us they're getting married. Will they wait until late next year?"

Ada chuckled, her eyes twinkling with mirth. "Why don't you ask them?"

Wilma playfully swatted Ada's arm. "Oh, hush. Let them take their time. But it seems like things are getting increasingly serious between them."

"They're good for each other," Wilma said, a contented smile on her face.

Ada nodded. "Yes, they are. It's a joy to see young love like that. Reminds me of my younger days."

"Younger days?" Samuel remarked, entering the living room with a chuckle, arriving just in time for supper. "I'd say our love is still as young as ever, Ada."

Ada turned to her husband with a playful smile. "Oh, Samuel, you always know just what to say. How did you sneak in? Where's the horse and buggy?"

"Out there." Samuel pointed out the window.

"Oh, I didn't even hear you."

"We must've been too busy talking, Ada."

As Jed and Krystal entered, their faces lit up with smiles, bringing fresh energy into the home. The couple greeted Wilma, Ada, and Samuel warmly. After that, Eli arrived and was invited to stay for a meal.

Supper preparations began, with Wilma and Ada moving around the kitchen and Jed and Krystal setting the table. Samuel stayed in the living room with Eli. Wilma was sad that Levi wasn't there to sit with them.

She kept her mind busy talking about their fun at the markets. Krystal shared some funny stories of what happened at the quilt store.

CHAPTER 35

*L*ater, throughout the meal, Wilma and Ada observed the couple discreetly.

"Jed, you've become quite the regular here," Ada commented with a smile. "You and Krystal make quite the team."

Jed grinned a hint of blush on his cheeks. "I enjoy the company, and the food is always great."

Krystal added, "And it's nice to have a change of scenery from our usual routines."

Samuel joined in on the observations about Jed and Krystal. "You two seem to be getting along quite well. It's a wonderful thing to see."

Jed responded, "Thank you, Samuel. Krystal's been a great friend. And, well, more than that. We've never made any secret of our feelings."

Krystal blushed but nodded in agreement, her hand finding Jed's under the table.

Samuel, with a knowing look, turned to his wife

and Wilma. "Looks like we might be hearing good news from these two before long."

Ada laughed. "That's what we've been saying, but we're not pushing them. Right, Wilma?"

"Absolutely," Wilma agreed.

"Let love take its course. Sometimes it has to take time," Eli commented.

The conversation then drifted to other topics, with Samuel sharing news from his day and asking about the happenings at the market stall. Wilma and Ada filled him in, their voices animated as they spoke again about their success at tea selling.

As dessert was served, a homemade pie Wilma had baked, Samuel shared his anecdotes, adding to the evening's cheerful mood. "When I first started courting Ada, I was so nervous. On our first date, I accidentally drove the buggy into a ditch."

The room erupted in laughter, with Ada playfully scolding him. "Samuel, you've told that story a hundred times!"

"But it never gets old," Samuel replied with a grin. "Everyone loves hearing about it."

Ada held her neck. "He gave me whiplash."

After the laughter died, Krystal asked, "What about you, Wilma? How did you meet Favor's father?"

"My mother pushed me to bring Josiah a pie, and then we fell in love that very day."

"That's romantic. I never knew," Krystal said.

"I don't often talk about him."

Krystal's eyes grew wide. "And what happened with you and Levi? How did you fall in love?"

Wilma put down her fork and hesitated. "It was slower. I didn't realize… it was just slower."

Ada looked over at Eli, expecting him to talk about his dear late wife and how they fell in love, but he didn't say a word. Oddly, he didn't pounce on the chance to speak about Frannie. Months ago, Frannie was every second word out of his mouth. "Anything to say, Eli?"

He looked up. *"Jah.* This apple pie is great, Wilma."

Ada raised her eyebrows in surprise and kept staring at him. "That's right, Eli. You won that apple pie contest with Frannie's recipe."

"That's right. But yours, Wilma, I'm sure this is the best apple pie I've ever tasted."

Wilma giggled like a girl at the comment, but Ada was unconvinced that his comment was genuine. Something didn't add up with Eli. She'd store it in the back of her mind.

After dinner, as they all relaxed with cups of tea, the conversation turned to Debbie and how quiet the house was without her and Jared.

The evening wound down, and Jed left, followed by Samuel, Ada, and Eli. The only people in the house were Wilma and Krystal.

"It's so quiet now," Wilma said as she sat on the couch.

Krystal settled beside her. "I know. It's weird without Debbie and Jared here."

"When you get married, it'll be just me and Red unless you and Jed decide to live here. You can do that until you get your own place. Stay for as long as you want."

"Would you mind if we did that?" Krystal asked.

"Mind? I'd love it. I only have Joy and Hope here now since the others moved away. There is Bliss and Florence, but I mean out of my six girls. Oh, I'm talking too much. I'm just trying to say that I consider you one of my girls. I'd love you to stay as long as possible."

"Thank you, Wilma. That means more than you know." Krystal leaned over and gave Wilma a hug.

CHAPTER 36

A few days later, Gabe visited Debbie at her new cottage, bringing a sizeable, sturdy basket half-filled with firewood.

"What have you got there?" Debbie asked as she opened the door for him.

He lifted the basket. "I thought you might be low on wood."

"I am." Debbie watched him enter her quaint living room, his eyes immediately gravitating towards the nearly empty woodpile beside the fireplace.

"You're running low. The logs I brought won't last more than a week or so," Gabe observed, placing the basket down.

While tidying up, Debbie felt embarrassed as she glanced at the meager pile. "Yes, I've been meaning to get more, but I haven't had the chance."

"I can borrow a cart and go get you some. You can't run out of firewood at this time of year."

"No, it's fine. I can arrange to get some."

"It's no trouble at all, Debbie. I want to help. Why don't you come with me?"

Debbie was pleased she had something to fill in her day—something that didn't involve unpacking.

Debbie agreed, and together they set out. Their first stop was Fairfax's place to exchange the horse and buggy for a sturdier horse and a wagon. Fairfax directed them to a reliable place to buy firewood.

The journey was filled with light-hearted conversation as they made their way to the firewood supplier.

"So, Debbie, got any more plans for the cottage?" Gabe asked, steering the horse along the scenic road.

Debbie smiled, looking out at the passing fields. "Well, I've been thinking about adding a shelf in the kitchen. For herbs, you know. I love cooking with fresh herbs rather than dried ones."

"That sounds great. Hopefully, the weather will be warm soon, and those we planted will grow and multiply. There's nothing like fresh herbs to liven up a meal. I could help you with that shelf."

"Oh, would you?" Debbie's eyes lit up. "I'd appreciate that. I'm not much of a carpenter, to be honest."

Gabe chuckled. "Consider it done. Do you have a favorite herb?"

Debbie thought for a moment. "I think basil. Its aroma always reminds me of summer."

Debbie laughed, enjoying the simplicity of the moment.

"I love fresh basil. It's amazing in so many dishes," Gabe commented.

"Do you cook much?"

"Not as much as I'd like," Gabe replied, eyes on the road ahead. "But I can make a mean spaghetti sauce. What about you?"

"I'm pretty passionate about cooking," Debbie said, her hands folded. "I've got some family recipes I'm eager to try out here. This cottage I've moved into, I want to make it a cozy, inviting place, you know?"

"That sounds great. What kind of dishes?"

Debbie thought for a moment, her gaze on the passing scenery. "Well, this chicken pot pie recipe has been in my family for ages. It's always a hit."

"I'd love to try that sometime," Gabe said warmly. "There's nothing better than a home-cooked meal. I've been getting spoiled with food staying with the bishop. But if I'm going to stay around, I'll need a place of my own."

Debbie was delighted to hear it.

Their conversation meandered as they rode along. They shared their favorite recipes, some successful and others ending in culinary disasters.

Gabe's responses were thoughtful, and he shared a few anecdotes, including a particularly humorous attempt at baking bread. The buggy moved steadily, the rhythmic clip-clop of the horse's hooves a soothing backdrop to their laughter and chatter.

Upon arriving at the firewood supplier, Gabe and Debbie were greeted by the owner, a robust man with a friendly demeanor. Gabe took the lead. "Good morning. I'm Gabe, and this is Debbie. We're here to pick up some firewood."

The owner shook their hands warmly, his eyes lingering curiously on Debbie. As he helped them load the cart, he casually remarked, "You're Amish, right? Your name's Debbie?" His tone was more of realization than a question.

Debbie, taken aback by his directness, nodded cautiously. "Yes, that's right."

Then, a look of recognition dawned on the man's face. "Wait a minute, aren't you the same Debbie who got left at the altar? My wife was telling me about it. She returned from the farmers' market with a whole bunch of tea and couldn't stop talking about it."

Debbie felt a sudden rush of panic; her personal story had become a topic of conversation for strangers. "Yes, that's me," she replied hesitantly. "But how did you hear about it?"

The owner continued, "My wife loves going to that market. She returned one day with this tea and said it was two older ladies helping out. She mentioned they told her about a young woman named Debbie who had a tough break. She said it was quite the story, and that's why we ended up with so much tea."

"Do you know why they told your wife about me?"

"No idea. But your tea is great. I'm not much of a tea drinker, or I wasn't until I started drinking Her Hopeful Heart."

Debbie was shocked. "Her Hopeful Heart?"

"Yes. The name of one of your tea blends. Seems pretty fitting to your situation, wouldn't you say?"

Debbie bit her lip, feeling a surge of emotions. Her heartache had become a selling point, a story for others to share and discuss. She glanced at Gabe, searching for some support or reassurance.

CHAPTER 37

Sensing Debbie's discomfort, Gabe quickly steered the conversation back to the business at hand. "We appreciate the help with the firewood. Debbie's been needing to restock for a while."

Thankfully, the owner took the hint and shifted his focus back to loading the cart, filling the awkward silence with talk about the quality of the wood and the mildness of the weather so far this winter season.

As they left the firewood supplier, the ride home was marked by a heavy silence. Debbie was lost in thought, her mind replaying the conversation with the owner.

Gabe, sensing her distress, finally broke the silence.

"Debbie, I had no idea they were talking about you at the market," he said, his voice filled with concern. "Perhaps that man's wife overheard something."

Debbie looked out at the passing countryside, her

heart heavy. "Maybe. It's... it's just so personal, and to think strangers are discussing it over tea..."

Gabe nodded. "It might've been a one-off thing," he suggested tentatively. "Or maybe Wilma and Ada didn't realize how far the story would spread. I wouldn't worry about it too much."

"But it's my story, Gabe. My life. It shouldn't be a topic for gossip or a sales pitch. It's... it's just not right. I don't like confrontations, but I must say something to them."

Gabe reached over, placing a reassuring hand on her arm. "I know, Debbie. And you're right. Maybe you should talk with them about it. Let them know how you feel."

"I should. I don't want to cause them any distress, though. They were trying to help in their way."

Gabe's expression softened. "Debbie, it's okay to set boundaries, even with friends. They care about you, they'll understand. I learned to set boundaries in my family a long time ago."

His words gave her a new perspective, but addressing the issue felt daunting.

When they arrived back at Debbie's cottage, Gabe helped unload the firewood, stacking it neatly in a corner of the small barn.

"Thanks, Gabe," Debbie said, her voice a little stronger now. "For everything today."

Gabe gave her a gentle smile. "Anytime, Debbie. And if you need someone to talk to about the market thing or anything else, you know where to find me."

Debbie smiled. "I might just take you up on that."

After Gabe left, Debbie sat by her newly replenished fireplace. The flames crackled and danced, providing a soothing backdrop to her turbulent thoughts. She knew a conversation with Wilma and Ada was inevitable. It was time to reclaim her story, to ensure that her personal journey wasn't reduced to entertainment for others.

CHAPTER 38

That night after Jared had gone to bed, Debbie sat alone, contemplating the conversation she needed to have with Ada and Wilma. The fire crackled softly as she mulled over their use of her personal story at the market. She rehearsed what to say, picturing their faces—Ada's earnest eyes, Wilma's kind smile—and felt her chest tighten.

The more Debbie thought about confronting them, the more she hesitated. How could she express disapproval to those who had only shown her kindness?

As the hours ticked by, Debbie's resolve waned. The risk of hurting Ada and Wilma weighed heavily on her. She realized she might not be able to have that conversation after all. Perhaps it was best to let it go, to accept that her life had become a sad tale, however uncomfortable it was.

Deciding against the confrontation, Debbie stood up from her fireside contemplation, feeling at peace.

She would live through the gossip. She'd been through worse.

That night, as she lay in bed, her decision to remain silent rested in her heart—a choice made out of love and respect for the two women who had been her steadfast support. Sometimes, silence was the unspoken price for harmony in the intricate web of community life.

A smile came to Debbie's lips as she thought of the names Ada and Wilma had made up for her tea. Her Hopeful Heart, New Beginnings Blend, Resilience Brew. Now that she'd found out what they'd been doing—the tales they'd been telling, all those names made sense. Debbie saw the humorous side. Ada and Wilma certainly had good imaginations.

CHAPTER 39

Ada and Wilma were enjoying a quiet day at Wilma's house. They had just cleared the lunch dishes when the sound of a car rolling up the driveway caught their attention.

Curious, they both hurried outside to see who their unexpected visitor might be. As the car came to a stop, they were surprised to see Mercy stepping out.

Wilma rushed over to her. "Mercy, what are you doing here? Is everything alright?"

Mercy hung her head. "No, it's not. I've left Stephen. We had a huge fight."

Before Ada and Wilma could process this revelation or respond, Mercy flounced past them into the house. Meanwhile, the driver retrieved a large suitcase from the trunk, set it on the porch with a thud, and then drove away, leaving a cloud of dust swirling in his wake.

Ada and Wilma exchanged a quick, bewildered glance before hurrying inside after Mercy. They found her in the living room, sinking heavily into an armchair.

Wilma was the first to speak. "Mercy, you're pregnant. Why in the world would you leave him?"

Mercy let out a sigh. "I'm just so tired, *Mamm*. I don't want to talk about it right now."

Ada stepped forward. "Mercy, dear, you know you can talk to us."

"Thanks, Ada. Maybe later. Right now, I'm just... I'm starving."

Wilma nodded understandingly, though her mind was still racing with questions and concerns. "Alright, dear. I'll fix you something to eat. You rest here."

As Wilma headed to the kitchen, Ada sat beside Mercy, wondering what to say.

In the kitchen, Wilma rubbed her neck, a mix of stress and concern knotting her muscles. Then she moved about, pulling ingredients from the fridge and pantry. Mercy had left her husband. It was unthinkable. What would people say?

The situation was unexpected and troubling. Wilma worried about the implications of Mercy's sudden departure on Mercy's other two children and her husband, especially considering her pregnancy.

Meanwhile, Mercy and Ada sat quietly. The comfort of Wilma's home was a stark contrast to the turmoil Mercy had left behind. The reasons for her leaving Stephen remained locked within her, a tumult of emotions she wasn't ready to unpack.

Wilma returned with a plate of food, setting it down gently in front of Mercy. "Here you go. Eat up. You need to take care of yourself, for your sake and the baby's." Wilma then looked over at Ada. "I need your help with something."

"Sure." Ada pushed herself to her feet, and then both women hurried to the kitchen.

"What do I do now?" Wilma whispered.

"I don't know, but you shouldn't keep saying how lonely you'll be in the house when everyone moves out. Maybe *Gott* heard your words and thought you needed company."

Wilma shook her head. "That's not what I want. Mercy's not company. She's hard work."

"I know. She always has been." Ada looked up at the ceiling. "There is always a saying for life's situations."

Wilma sighed. "You like your little sayings. What is the saying for this one? Tell me if you think it will help."

"Appreciate what you have before time makes you appreciate what you had."

"Oh, you mean when I had peace away from Mercy's demands?" Wilma whispered.

"Exactly."

At that moment, they heard another car.

Ada's eyes bugged out. "I wonder if Stephen has followed her. That would be a romantic gesture that she can't ignore."

"Oh, it has to be him. Who else would it be?" Wilma's eyes lit up with hope as they both hurried to the door. On opening the door, they saw the bishop's wife from Cherish and Malachi's community.

"Isn't that Leonie, Bishop Zachariah's wife?" Ada asked.

"It is. Why is she here?" Wilma whispered.

"I have no idea."

"I'm sure she doesn't even like us," Wilma added.

"Jah, after you brought up that one of her adopted children might be Christina's child."

"I couldn't help that. The medication I was taking was affecting me."

Ada shook her head. "Well, that doesn't matter. The words came from your mouth."

Behind the bishop's wife was a young woman, an older teenager.

Wilma knew she'd have to say something, but no words came out.

Thankfully, Ada stepped forward. "Hello, Leonie. Nice of you to visit. We didn't know you were coming." Ada offered a huge smile.

A sour expression remained on Leonie's face as she looked at Wilma, who was standing behind Ada. "This was all your doing, Wilma." She turned around and waited for the young woman to catch up with her. Once she was beside her, Leonie announced, "This is Grace, and she's here to meet Christina, her birth mother."

Grace's mouth turned down at the corners as she corrected her adoptive mother. "I want to meet my 'real' mother."

Ada and Wilma just stood there, frozen like statues. Mercy squeezed in between them eating her sandwich. "What's this about?"

Wilma looked at Ada and whispered, "I know you don't have a saying for this situation."

Ada glanced at Mercy and then whispered back to Wilma, "It never rains, but it pours?"

"That sounds about right," Wilma mumbled, staring at the two women before her. Then Wilma forced a smile. "Lovely to see you both. Do come inside."

Just as all the women sat down in the living room, they heard the sounds of a horse and buggy pulling up outside. Ada got to her feet. "Don't worry, Wilma. No matter who they are, I'll tell them to come back another time."

"Denke, Ada."

"What's going on?" Mercy whispered to her mother.

As Wilma searched for words, Ada rushed back to her. "Wilma, you won't believe this. It's Obadiah. He's just pulled up outside."

Wilma's mouth fell open. "Are you sure?"

"Yes. He's here!"

Wilma staggered to her feet wondering what to do.

"Who's Obadiah? Will someone tell me what's going on?" Mercy looked down at her empty plate. "I could do with another sandwich."

Ada stared wide-eyed at Wilma. "And don't even ask. There are no sayings for this."

Thank you for reading Her Hopeful Heart.

For a downloadable/printable Series Reading Order of all Samantha Price's books, scan below or find it at: Samantha PriceAuthor.com

THE NEXT BOOK IN THE SERIES

The next book in the series is Book #41:
Return to Love's Promise

THE NEXT BOOK IN THE SERIES

The Baker family's generations-old apple orchard faces a season unlike any before. Three unexpected visitors bring a deluge of secrets and emotions, disrupting everything.
As these revelations unfold, love finds a way to blossom in the most unexpected of places.

ABOUT SAMANTHA PRICE

Samantha Price is a USA Today bestselling and Kindle All Stars author of Amish romance books and cozy mysteries. She was raised Brethren and has a deep affinity for the Amish way of life, which she has explored extensively with over a decade of research. She is mother to two pampered rescue cats, and a very spoiled staffy with separation issues.

www.SamanthaPriceAuthor.com

instagram.com/samanthapriceauthor
pinterest.com/AmishRomance
youtube.com/@samanthapriceauthor

Made in United States
Orlando, FL
21 March 2024